I0553387

Pacific Coast Highway

Jack Remick

Copyright © 2011 Jack Remick
Registration number: TXu 1-772-521
All rights reserved.
This is a work of fiction. There is no resemblance to anyone living or dead.
Published by Quartet Global Books
Contact: quartetglobal@gmail.com
Cover design ©2013 by Susan Canavarro
ISBN-13:978-0-9840493-4-9 (paperback)
ISBN:978-0-9840493-2-5 (e-book)

Published by Quartet Global

Seattle

Pacific Coast Highway

Those who know will forgive
the details if the story is right.

PCH BREAKDOWN

<u>BEATRICE</u>

<u>VIVIAN</u>

<u>MACKEY</u>

The Proposition

I sat in the pickup. Mel had the wheel. At two-thirty the house lights had been off for half an hour and Dr. Johnson's BMW 760Li lay in a shaft of light—yellow and blue and silver and glass. Dr. Cynthia Johnson was a long-legged, blonde-headed, silicon-queen surgeon who chopped the fat out of LA beauties and rebuilt them into sleek, smooth, big-boobed beach honeys.

Acid was chewing a hole in my gut so I shuffled through the glove box hunting for the Tums.

"Relax, Jonny," Mel said. "It's just a car."

"You do it then." I said.

I shook out three Tums and chewed them and waited until the burning cooled and then I stepped out of the pickup, strapped on the webbed tool belt with the electric screwdrivers and the socket set and the wire cutters.

Crossing under the light, my shoes crunched on the sandy concrete. I expected alarms to go off and lights to come on, but when I stopped there was just the thrum of swimming pool pumps and the faint buzz of the night. I slid under the 760, reached up into the fender panel and with the cutters, cut the by-pass I had patched in while the car was in the shop. The 760's alarm was now dead. After that, you could do anything to her you wanted. I keyed the car, opened the door and got behind the wheel.

Across the street, Mel started the pickup and drove away.

At the shop on Pacific Coast Highway, I ran the 760 into Bay 1 and shut her down.

I hated Mel right then. I hated the business Mel was in. I hated myself for letting Mel suck me into his penny-ante pissant crime scheme. In Bay 1 I would gut the 760. I would take her apart piece by piece down to the instrument panel until she lay spread out, butchered, her near-new parts gleaming raw bones in the neon overheads. At first it was easy, even a little bit of a thrill, but now, every time I cut into a car I got sick to my stomach.

While I slaughtered and boned the 760, while I waited for Mel to show up, I remembered the day he called me into his office. I was in the shop finishing up a rush chip job on an Audi TT. It was around

1

quitting time. Maybe 6:30. Mel was sitting at the metal desk, head down, like a man praying, but even then I knew Mel prayed to just three gods Money, Women, and Doobie.

He reared back, braced his smooth black clean shaven head between his thick hands and said, "Jonny, I'm gonna let you go."

"What? I'm not getting the work done?"

"You're getting the work done fine."

He got out of his chair, went to the shop window. Standing there he looked like he could tear the lug nuts off a BMW with his bare teeth. Mel's a big guy and if you look at just his size you'd cross the street before you'd brush up close to him. Out in the shop, the Audi TT was up on the rack, its electrics spread out like the guts of metal animal just butchered.

"What's going on then, dude?"

"Dude," he said, "no one's called me dude in a while."

"You're letting me go because I call you dude?"

"I'm going broke, Jonny."

"Broke?"

"Yeah. Broke. I'll close the shop if things don't shape up."

"You want me to work for free."

He laughed. He sat down in his chair, elbows on the desk, and he snapped open an Altoids mint box and fingered a rolled joint that he lit and took a hit on and he held the smoke in then let it out in short jerks. The pale smoke reminded me of mist rising up off the ocean.

"I need some help and it doesn't look like you're the man."

"What's eating you?"

He bogarted the joint, leaned back in his chair.

"I owe some people some money that I don't have and I can't get."

"I've got a few bucks," I said. "What do you need?"

"Eighty."

"Eighty. I can swing that."

"Eighty grand," he said.

I looked out the door of the shop to where the Audi TT sat in its Toledo blue crystal paint, smooth and sloped so you could almost see the wind splitting over the shell and I remembered once out on the Santa Monica freeway watching an 850CSi chase a Ferrari like a wolf after a calf, lights flashing, horn blaring and the BMW blew past. I was sitting on 120 but he made me look like I'd blown a piston and froze up the engine. There in the shop the TT looked like a blue arrow. I didn't know it was aimed at my heart. I looked at Mel. Then at the car.

"These sons of bitches want meat, Jonny. If they don't get their money they cut my nuts off and stuff'em in my mouth."

I looked at the sweat on his face, smelled his cannabis in the air.

I owed Mel. I'd owed him for a long time. He held out a hand to me when I didn't know a torque converter from a jackrabbit and he'd let me work overtime and gave clients who wanted me to chip their engines to tweak another fifty horsepower out of their stock mills. And then Mel glared at me.

"What?"

"I need a man who can use his tools in the right place at the right time and keep his mouth shut after he does it. Jonny, you know every secret code on these things."

You know how it is when you're in the dark and you feel something crawl up your back? That's the way it was when Mel looked at me then. I felt creepy. Crawly. Dirty.

I knew what he wanted all right, and I felt sacrilegious.

"What are you asking me, Mel?"

"I got a guy in TJ. He wants that TT. Wednesday morning."

"You want me to run that TT to Mexico?"

"He pays cash."

"You know what'll happen to it in TJ" I said. "They'll gut it and skin it and chop it for parts."

"Not this guy. He wants the car. Whole. Look, Jonny. You don't care. Mr Franz don't care, I don't give a shit. Insurance covers it all anyway."

I came back from TiJuana on a bus. I hadn't been on a bus in a long time. I took a taxi from the Greyhound to PCH. The taste of the Greyhound stayed in my mouth until I got a lungful of ocean breeze

Dr Johnson's 760 looked like Edward Scissorhands had chewed on it by the time Mel showed up. Grinning. Half-whacked. A joint glued to his lips. He walked around the 760 the way Patton did in that movie where he surveys the bodies in the desert after a tank battle.

"You're good, Jonny," he said. "Damn, you are good."

"This is the last one, Mel. I finish this one, I quit."

"It's not that easy, J Boy," he said.

Everything went to hell when he told me we were going to chop Ms Redman's 850 CSi.

I'm barely two months on Mel's payroll the first time I meet Beatrice Redman. I'm young and stupid so I don't know I'm on a cold slide to murder. You can't tell by looking. She drives her BMW 850 CSi into Mel's Shop on PCH. She's tall and thin. Black pants, black top, a white wrap you can almost see through. And you notice that she looks hungry. No big deal. A lot of women in LA look hungry.

BMW. Black. The back end has a ding the size of a football crushing in the BMW logo. I feel like someone's crushed me. Yanked my heart out. An 850CSi is as close to perfection as anything humans can ever make. I look at her. She smiles at me. A killer smile. She's hell on wheels. You get a woman's number just like that. You smell the hell-fire, see the ashes in the eyes, but you can't look away. You like fire. You want her to jam a smoldering cigarette to your nipple. Anything. It's going to hurt. So what? Simple.

"Who did this?"

"When can you have it fixed?"

"A couple of days," I say.

"You're new here, aren't you?"

"I'm new."

"What's your name?"

"Jonny Wattron. No H."

"Jonny. No H." She says it like it's a mouthful of cotton candy.

I check over the BMW. Run her through the computer.

58 Via Campesina, Palos Verdes Estates. 1996. 850 CSi. Only 38,000 miles. Not even a scuff on the accelerator and brake pedals. Leather smells almost new. As I do the paper work, I watch her. I try not to notice the quiver in the lips. The skin is tanned, but her face isn't lined. She's maybe 40, but like her car,

she's in good shape. The sun makes her glisten. The mileage makes her a mystery.

"Well, I think it's gonna run you close to two grand."

"What?" she says.

"About two grand. To fix this up. The insurance."

"I am my own insurance," she says. ""Should I just throw it away and buy a new one?" That smile again. Red mouth. White teeth. Very white teeth.

That was a Monday morning. Monday afternoon. I strip and patch the ding. The dent eats three layers of fiber glass before it smoothes out. Tuesday morning I sand and prime. Tuesday afternoon I match the midnight black from BMW. And paint it. Laying on the paint, watching it curve to the panel. A second coat of black and three coats of lacquer and you can't tell she ever backed into whatever it was she backed into. Wednesday afternoon I call her.

She answers. Asks if I can bring it out.

Mel says Ms Redman is good for it. He gives me taxi fare. We tack it on the bill.

We close Wednesday evening at 7:00. By 7:10 I'm driving PCH to Palos Verdes Estates. It's a cool night. Sunset already dying. You see the lights along

PCH like sparklers and the rusty layer of sky on the horizon, LA red—a burnt orange hovering over the black line of the Pacific Ocean. The air is still. It's paradise in the BMW. The CSi talks to me. All the way. I love cars that talk. Big. Fast. Powerful. Comfortable. Rich. Leather. The she-smell of perfume and money and the dull odor of cigarettes.

For a couple of beats I'm at a stoplight and I look at the car next to me and Miss Southern California smiles and I smile back and I know she doesn't blink if I'm in a Chevy or a Ford, even my chopped Ford. But an 850. Well.

I want it.

Palos Verdes Estates is everything LA should be—winding hill-side streets lined with eucalyptus trees and jacaranda and on the slopes, neo-Spanish castles built of white brick and red tile roofs that glisten in the sunset melting down over the Pacific Ocean.

When you turn a close curve, peacocks with their rainbow fans screech at you like they own the place.

Later she tells me about the peacocks—How someone let them loose and how they took over and now perch on rooftops and how they breed and how much she loves them and how if anyone killed one of them, she'd have him skinned alive. I pull into the drive at 58 Via Campesina, a curved drive big enough to hold a herd of German cars and I shut down the mill of the 850 CSi and I hear the birds chittering and the peacocks call and I hear the long slow whine of swimming pool pumps and somewhere, in another universe, a crow caws and for a second I forget who I am and where I am and what I am doing because for just that second I have a feeling for what it would be like to come to a place like that every day with its peacocks on the roof and a swimming pool that hums and inside a woman who wears black and white and drives a big fast powerful rich German machine. I think about home, the futon I sleep on, the breakfast of raisin bran and cold coffee. I get out of the car.

The garage door rolls up, a slow, mechanical chugging, and there, in front of a shiny black Jaguar stands Bea Redman in black pants and white blouse with a pearl choker. Her hair looks like the wings of a big bird.

She rubs her hand over the trunk lid. You see her skin mirrored in the lacquer. The woman and the car—sleek, smooth, dangerous. She looks at me. She says, "It looks like new." After she inspects the BMW, she stands back like an arts patron measuring the value of black and white in an expensive wall piece. She smells good. Fresh like a rose in high bloom wanting to be plucked.

"I don't see a car," she says.

"A car?"

"Take you back?"

"I'll grab a taxi," I say.

"Nonsense. I'll drive you."

"It's okay," I say. "You already paid for the cab."

She laughs. "I suppose I did. But it's the Jag. I want you to listen. It's making a new sound."

"What kind of sound?"

"It's a very low growl, like a moan."

She talks at me as she drives. Easy. Like we're friends from a long time back. On the way she points out places where her family built the first Redman Markets that later became Quality Foods that later became Safeway stores when Safeway squeezed out of Seattle to milk the LA cash cow.

"My family fed LA for 70 years," she says.

Money. It oozes out of her. It's like oil seeping out of the ground. It's there like air, like water, like blood. It's the first time I've even been that close to that much money. She tells me stuff I don't need to know. Stuff I don't want to know. But, it's her Jag. I'm the mechanic. I listen. I feel the leather seat. Smell the cigarette smoke. Santa Monica Freeway. The 850. Zing.blow the doors off everything. One hundred and fifty, flat out until you die or have to stop for gas. She throttles along at thirty. A shame. A car meant to cruise at one-ten.

At the shop, when I get out, she looks at me like she doesn't want to let me go.

"Thanks again," she says. Leans down, eyes on my eyes.

"You're a pretty fancy chauffeur, Ms Redman."

"You're awfully formal. Call me Beatrice."

She says it like an Italian. Bea-tree-che.

"That's a nice name," I say. "Oh, Ms Redman.Beatrice."

"Yes?"

"Your engine's okay."

"I'm sorry?"

"That strange noise in the engine? Nothing wrong I can hear."

"It's always like that isn't it? You take it in and it's okay."

Redman money buys me a steak and a pound of Starbuck's Espresso grind for in the morning.

Mel tosses the key to Ms Redman's 850 CSi at me and tells me to go get it that night and to cut it down by Saturday.

I tell him I won't do it.

He tells me I'll do it.

This isn't just another car. I'm mad and hungry. I don't want to do it. I want to quit. I want to go write poetry. I want to be a poet. But I don't know anything about poetry and I do know a lot about cars like Audis and Mercedes and BMWs and I know that the BMW 850 CSi is the most perfect automobile ever built. V-12, 296 bhp, six speed manual transmission, so smooth when you hit sixth gear at 120 there's still enough oomph in her to jerk your head back and I know you don't treat an 850 like a sports car because it's not a sports car. It weighs five thousand pounds and when you brake at top speed she comes back smooth, straight as a steel rod, without shimmy or shiver or wobble or dance the way a mortal machine does. And I know you don't chop an 850 CSi. You just don't.

I'd been around cars all my life but I never felt close to god till that day I sat in Beatrice Redman's 850 CSi. Some metal is metal. Some leather is leather. Some walnut is just walnut but when the engineers put all that together in the 850, they built a machine that's like Leonardo DaVinci crossing paths with Werner Von Braun and the two of them shaking hands with Albert Einstein and for one second there is perfection in the world but it's like the universe can't stand that kind of competition and so they had to quit making the 850 in 1997, the whole 800 series came to an end and all that was left of perfection I would gut in Mel's Body Shop on PCH. No. People like Mel can't stand perfection so they cut it up. Into little pieces. And sell it a piece at a time.

"That's an 850, Mel," I say.

"Jonny, it's just a car."

"It's an 850," I say. "How many of these have you seen in your life?"

"Exactly two," he says.

"Yeah, well, I'm not gonna do it."

He looks like I'd pulled his eye teeth.

"Jonny," he says, "I'll never understand you. What do you want?"

I had to think about that for a couple of seconds and then I say, "Uncle Big taught me one lesson, Mel, you don't tear up the good things 'cause there aren't many of them."

"Piss on your Uncle Big. What are you saying?"

"I'm saying I can't do this anymore."

"Sounds like more of your Okie bullshit to me."

He draws the drawer of his metal desk, sets out the Altoid mint box, opens it, pulls out one of his rolled joints, lights it, inhales a lungful and holds it, then lets it out in slow jerks.

"Yeah," he says, "I always knew there was something wrong with you, Jonny. A man won't even share weed with a guy, you know. I seen jerk-offs like you in the League. Come outta nowhere thinking they're better'n anybody, but they's really just warmed over dog shit."

"You're stoned, Mel."

"Sure I'm stoned and I'm gonna stay stoned."

"When you talk shit like that I want to bust your face."

"Go ahead. Go ahead, do it."

He stands. Wobbles a bit. Then he lips the joint. Smoke bends up into his eyes like a gray snake. I laugh at him.

"You know what, Mel? I quit. I'm taking my tools and I'm outta here."

He balls his fists up like an old time street fighter and he rocks back and forth on his heels and he says, "Come on you punk ass little chicken shit cocksucker, come on."

I turn my back on him.

"Come on, shit head. Come on. Do it. Take a swing."

I leave him in the shop. I go out. Pick up my socket set, wipe it clean with a red cloth, rub down the box ends and the mallets, set the tools in the box, lock the box, and roll it out of the garage while Mel stands rocking back and forth, fists still balled, eyes still squinted, smoke still drifting up and over his black shaven head.

"If you walk out that door, asshole I'll mess you up so bad."

"Sure, Mel," I say.

I close the door, take a deep breath, roll the tool box to my Ford and open her up and it's been a long time since I had a full set of tools in her and she groans as I hoist the box off its caster and set it in and then I set the caster alongside the box. I look back. Mel stands in the doorway reeling.

"I'll get you, you little shit. I know where you live."

"I'll be back tomorrow for my check," I say.

"It won't be here." He slams the door. Glass rattles.

I open the Ford, settle behind the wheel. Where am I going now?

It's a slow drive up PCH. The night is clear with just the dusting of an ocean mist. Out over the Pacific, white crests to lines as waves boil up then disappear on the sand. Dark.

My apartment sits like a vacant face waiting for enlightenment. I sit in the Ford listening to her pop and cool down and I remember reading an ad for a BMW mechanic at Saar's Foreign Auto but if I go looking for work it's back to square one and I remember the first day I drove down out of the Valley, over the Grapevine curled down past Santa Clarita down to the sea. I haven't come far in three years. First stop, Mel's shop. Second stop I stumble into a place in Venice and I go back and forth between the two ever since. A new job means I give up the gravy I get stripping cars for Mel. A new job means wages, just wages, and then what?

I roll my tools back inside the apartment. Sit on a worn out sofa, look at a dinky 12 inch TV that's lopsided with bad sound and listen to the rumble of a fridge about to turn in forever.

When I wake up, I remember a little dream—in the dream there's a tall woman wearing black pants and driving a black BMW. Her hair splays like wings that kind of swoop out because her head wants to fly away off her body and I'm broken out in a sweat and I check my watch and it's 3 a.m. and the TV is still on and the picture is still lopsided, and the sound is still rotten and for a second I'm lost, about as lost as I've ever been and there's nothing I can do about it.

I don't like it in-between, but here I am in-between. Stuck. Can't go back to Mel, can't go forward into nothing and I understand something about myself then, kind of like the feeling I had when I found Uncle Big dead in his bed, his belly swelled up and his tongue poked out of his mouth. I understand that maybe I am one of those guys who is always in-between, always leaving one place, never getting to the next one, one of those guys whose life is just waiting to die. The next day around 6:00 I drive back to the shop. It's closed up tight. No lights. No Mel. No check. Inside, it still smells like patchouli but there's a scorched leather smell. Someone's been torching the inside of a car. But I don't care now. What I do care about is the money Mel owes me. Rent money. Gas money. Food money.

I go back out to my Ford. My Ford. Chrome header plugs, chopped top, lowered front end, a throw-back to the 50's because if you know, it's a show piece. Something special. Something no one else has. You got that, you got something. The lope of the 450 horse mill tells you it's built. Wide-track tires, a ton of chrome—my understated way.

Beatrice Redman's 850CSi is parked beside my Ford. Sure. Like nothing can surprise me.

"Wow," she says. "This yours?"

"Yes ma'am."

"I thought we'd agreed you'd call me Beatrice."

"I still can't get my tongue around all that," I tell her. She laughs.

"Instead of punishing you, why don't I take you out to dinner?"

She says it casual. Like it's nothing. Like yeah. Sure. Like take your pal to lunch. Why not. Like everybody in LA does it. Like where is Mel?

She gets us a table at a place called Casa del Sol in Marina Del Rey. Beatrice knows the waiter and the maître d' and they call her Ms Redman. I smell money under the scent of grilled mahi-mahi and baked Brie and whole roasted garlic.

Beatrice eats a spinach salad, a piece of grilled white fish. Half a slice of crusty bread dipped in olive oil and balsamic vinegar. A lot of white wine.

In the light I watch her. She's a knot in my gut as she hits the second bottle of Marcusa Soave. If I hit the bottom of two bottles of wine at one meal I'm face down in the chocolate mousse. With her, it shows just a light flushing in her cheeks.

We finish in silence then she says, "You need a job, don't you?"

"Yeah, well. Mel and me, we had a little falling out."

"I need someone to drive me to Cabo tomorrow."

"I'm a mechanic."

"I don't like to do Mexico alone."

"I've gotta look for work."

"Mel won't take you back. You know that."

"Because of your 850?"

"What?"

"You know about your car, right?"

"I don't know what you're talking about. I told him that if you stayed, he'd have to find another place."

"What do you mean, find another place?"

"I own that property," she says.

"Is that right?"

"Yes or no?"

"For how long?"

"As long as you like," she says.

"Are you taking the Jag or the 850?"

She looks at me, eyes sparkling, lips red, like she can see through all forty layers of bullshit down to the hunger. And then she says the 850 of course.

I don't know how to handle it. I've never met a woman like this, a woman who buys what she wants then looks you in the eye and smiles and dares you to find your way back to where you come from.

At first it feels good to be bought. No one ever wanted me enough to slap money on the table. I feel myself stepping into a very large steel trap. What's weird is I like the bite of the teeth against my ankle. Pain does stuff to your groin.

"A man's got to eat," I say.

She covers my hand with hers. A big smile.

"You won't regret a thing," she says.

Cabo

Bea Redman is a lot like her 850 CSi. Black hair, smooth skin, a flash of color at the throat, a sleek look to her as if she's in motion standing still, as if the wind rushes to her just so it can feel itself flow over her for a second before it dies the way a mantis dies when his female sucks him dry then chews off his head.

Bea has a kind of power to her like a V-12 hitting on all cylinders at 150 MPH, and I imagine her at idle speed all that torque all those RPMs waiting, a coiled spring, a snake, a cannon loaded and primed just itching for the match, so it's easy to say yes when she asks me to drive her to Cabo.

I'd have driven her to hell to get behind the wheel of that 850, to feel it hot and surging under my hands. She laughs when she sees my fingers caress the wheel—walnut like brown skin oiled and wet, the hide of a tree sacrificed to the god of speed.

"Go ahead, take it to the limit, but you pay for your own tickets."

"I'll die happy," I say.

A flat Mexican highway. 140. The 850 seethes over the pavement, the sound of her V-12, the hiss and whine of rubber skimming the blacktop and the occasional click of Bea's gold lighter as she lights another Diabolique, her imported Moroccan cigarettes with the gold tip and the tobacco that smells as sweet as the 850 feels when I pump her up to 150 and hold her there and she runs so smooth I can set a coin on the dash and it won't budge.

Bea sits in the slice of sun cutting through the open sunroof and she strokes her legs, legs the color of hot caramel.

"What are you looking at," she asks me.

"Just driving."

"Not my legs?"

"You have nice legs."

"They cost a lot." She laughs.

"How's that?"

"Mud baths, massage, depilatories."

"Depilatories?"

"Hair removal." She rubs the golden calves. "This isn't natural."

The 850 generates horsepower. A man gets used to its smoothness through the range from 90 up. At 140, still smooth, rich. And something left if you want it.

"You like cars better than you like women, don't you?"

"I understand cars," I say.

She laughs. The ice breaks.

Me. An 850. 130 miles an hour. Sun roof. Hot weather. I mean...

Beatrice wallows in the sun the way an iguana does, head back, like she sucks food and energy from the rays. Legs stretched out, the woman and the car. A lot of leg. A lot of car.

She runs her hand from thigh to ankle and I touch the accelerator, take the 850 up to 150 and still it purrs and says go ahead Jonny, see if I have a limit and Bea rocks back in the leather and rests her black head on the crash pad and her neck looks like the smooth side of a piece of suede and she glances at me and then leans over and points at the tach and smiles and says "Do you like it, Jonny? Do you like the way it feels?'

I ease down to 140, foot trembling on the accelerator.

She says, "It just sucks up gas at that speed, we'll have to stop soon."

She touches me on the shoulder and I shiver in the Mexican heat, against the warm wet leather of the most perfect automobile ever built.

"Not many cars can run that hot that long."

"You haven't even taken her over the top, Jonny."

I look at myself in her shades, see my white T-shirt in the lenses. See the ruby red wet lips and the tan skin.

"How much more is there left in her?

"I pegged her once at 180 but we had a tail wind coming off the Grapevine."

"That's downhill," I say.

"Oh she'll do it in the flat too. Pull into the next Pemex?"

She looks out the window. I let her slide back to 120, 110. At 100 the BMW feels like we've come to a full stop. At 50 I could step out and walk beside her.

I haul up for gas. The engine, in the 110 degree heat, doesn't even creak but I still let her idle for a minute just to hear the sweet hum of contentment.

"Why don't you fill up. I have to make a pit stop."

"Pit stop. Now you talk like a guy."

"You think so, Jonny? I'd love to talk like a guy."

"One thing."

She looks at me. "Yes?"

"Credit card? Cash?"

She leans in, opens the glove box, hands me five thousand pesos.

Beatrice lights a Diabolique with the gold lighter she keeps in a black velvet pouch and when the cigarette is burning, she tucks the lighter away.

"You don't smoke," she says.

"Bad for you."

"You avoid everything that's bad for you?"

"If I can help it. Like breathing smog."

"About Mel," she says. "How did you feel about working for a black man?"

"I don't have any trouble with that. I didn't want to work for him anymore anyway. He voted for the Bushes."

"Everyone in my family voted for the Bushes," she says.

"No one in my family ever voted."

"You drive like you've been in a Beamer all your life."

"You call it a Beamer?"

"Don't mechanics call it that?"

"I call it a car."

"Very generic," she says. "Very simple."

She doesn't know I just saved her BMW from death.

The sun in Cabo, hot rich Mexican sun, spikes into the skin and leaves a little message deep down. Beatrice lies on the pool deck, spectacular, smooth, hot skin oiled. I wait for her to make her move. All the way down I've waited. Nothing. Maybe all she wanted was a chauffeur. I kiss Mel good-bye to become a livery boy for the Oily Rich.

I suck down half a dozen margaritas and whip up the seventh when she opens her eyes and says, "Careful, Jonny. Don't want you unable to perform."

Dinner is beefsteak and frutas del mar and saffron rice and flan bathing in caramel sauce and then brandy.

After dinner we walk on the beach. Beatrice lets me know she's the boss. "Have you ever tied a woman to a bed post before having your way with her?" she asks me.

"I've never had my way with a woman," I say.

"Good. I like new toys."

The house stands high up on a mound, white, bright chrome brilliance, red tile roof, red brick walk ways, a carpet of ice plant flowers. From the bedroom we look out on the Sea of Cortez.

"Don't talk," she rasps, her whiskey baritone serious now. "Don't talk to me when we're naked unless I tell you to."

The first time is always a mess even when you know what you're doing. But you'll remember the first time. Years later you'll remember it. You forget act two, the middle, and you sometimes forget the end, but you always remember the beginning. Especially with a woman who knows what she wants. Beatrice knew what she wanted. And she told me how to do it.

Beatrice's biological clock beats to its own sweet rhythm, sex, sleep, eat, walk on the beach, sex, lunch, ceviche and sweet tortillas—walk on the beach, sex, drive to town for tequila, tecate, sex, walk on the beach at sunset, sex, sleep.

At the end of the week, I'm not just an employee, not just a driver, I'm something else, something I've never been. For the first time in my life, I'm with a woman who stalks men. Uses them. Takes what she wants. I didn't know what that meant.

Then.

Back in LA we run by my place in Venice. She smokes a Diabolique behind dark glasses as I pack a few things in a black suitcase with a broken latch—my one piece of real luggage—Mr. Safeway provides the rest. I stack jeans and T-shirts in bags in the trunk of the 850. Beatrice writes a check, leaves it on the bed. "For the landlord," she says.

"My tools," I say.

"I'll send someone to get them," she says.

That was the beginning.

Books

After Cabo Beatrice sits out by the pool reading. She gives me the run of the house on Via Campesina. There are things everywhere. Paintings on the walls, objects on small nested wooden tables. Nothing chrome or plastic, but expensive things that get better with age. Dark subtle objects lost in time, jerked out of their time, objects brought through time like spears. Exotic bird feathers. Feather masks. Leather cups. Beads carved from bone. A table built of ebony and goatskin.

And Beatrice reads. Surrounded by all these objects, she reads novels by men I've never heard of... Alain Robbe Grillet, Michel Butor, Samuel Beckett. Heinrich Boll. Gunther Grass. One day she puts down her book.

"You don't read, do you Jonny?"

"Maps and menus and repair manuals," I say.

She leads me to the library. The lower room beyond the guest room with the rose wallpaper and the huge stuffed alligator. So quiet in the library. Quieter than any place I have ever been in my life, it is a cathedral for books.

She shows me books made with leather bindings and gold lettering, books two hundred years old with wrinkled leather covers. Books about history, books about Rome and Greece and the Maya who built stone cities. Dead men and living women—Rosellen Brown, Margaret Atwood, Susan Sontag. She handles the books the way you handle nitro—gently, delicately, lovingly, carefully.

Beatrice has read them all. New books come once a week. She reads them. Out by the pool.

At first I just watch her on the deck chair, the hum of the pool filter like a time machine. She wears dark glasses, the way she did in Cabo. Mysterious. Even in bed. Black bikini and white wrap. She sips wine, red wine, white wine, gold wine, pink wine, good wine, as she turns her pages. An occasional breeze flutters the wrap, stirs up the blood.

I don't know how many men have studied a woman reading. The way she moves her lips, her hands, the way she raises the knee to scratch. There is something otherworldly about that scratch. And the back of the naked thigh. Something urgent, primitive.

Beatrice read, I watched.

And then, in the silence of the night, after she was exhausted, after I'd tied her up and eaten her until she screamed, after she'd come like a banshee howling, after the sweat and the sobbing, after she was asleep, I'd go to the library to read. Alone. In quiet secret.

It's hard getting your head to go from Turlock to LA to Balzac's Paris. Balzac, I'd never heard of Balzac and I knew Paris was in

France, but where was France? France was in Europe. Germany was in Europe. In Germany they built BMWs.

I read until my eyes burned and blurred and I read until I discovered why she read. There was vision in reading. One writer said that if you want to learn new things, read old books. My family was there in *The Grapes of Wrath* right down to Uncle Big. I had to read about them to know where I came from. And it didn't make me happy. Where I came from.

Books.

Mornings, I put them away, at first, but when I saw that she enjoyed knowing I read, I left them out, to show her. The more I read, the more I wanted to be in her. To show her.

After morning sex, Bea swam laps for an hour.

A serious swimmer.

The rhythm didn't vary—read, sex, swim, eat, sex, read, swim, dinner. The more we have sex, the younger she gets.

When we needed something, either we shopped together or she called out for delivery. Money does that. Just call someone. Forget bargains.

At the wine shop, she taught me about Spanish wine, French wine, Hungarian wine, Napa Valley wine, and wines from sandy soils so rare no one labeled the bottles so each came with a number on the bottom, each bottle costing a week's salary pulling spark plugs for Mel.

Beatrice the cook shows me secrets of Chinese, French, Armenian.

Sauce, the secret is in the sauce, the marinade, the juice. Juice.

"A good friend, Linda Dagdigian," she says, "the best Armenian cook ever. Taught me to make <u>dolma</u> the right way." Dolma. Currants, pine nuts. I watch grape leaves and ground lamb become finger food. Magic. A long way from pinto beans out of a can and black strap dribbled on dry cornbread. You get like that. Old tastes turn to shame on your tongue. Money gives your taste buds a new sense of urgency. More. New. Bettah.

Skin Worms

Then one Monday, a year ago, after a pretty hard week-end where we didn't get out of bed for more than ten minutes at a time, I

18

looked at Beatrice on the deck. She was wearing her black and white bikini with the see through wrap that is like a diaphanous cloud. Diaphanous. You can't pin this woman down.

With anything definite.

In the afternoon sun I looked up and the sun slanted over the roof and it hit her full on.

She was reading. Marquez.

As she turned the page, a shaft of sunlight x-rayed through her face and neck silhouetting the scars under the skin.

Dozens of them.

Little sutures where some magician took old wrinkles and tried to turn them into soft young skin.

A flood hit me. I wondered, Jesus. How old is she really? I'd never asked. Didn't need to know. Was afraid to know.

She turned to look at the sun like it bothered her and she was going to order it to go away or to buy it or peel a few years off her skin. I felt claws tear at me.

A huge cockroach. An insect. She wasn't young and beautiful. Her skin wasn't soft and pliant. Was this the woman I'd been balling for four years? Why?

I remembered the day in Casa del Sol in Marina del Rey when she told me she owned Mel's place and I remembered the drive to Cabo San Lucas when I gave in, no questions because of the way she said it. I wanted it and I remembered the way she looked at me in Cabo the first time. She looked at me, waiting. The cruel curve of her lips made me bow my head when she told me no talking until she said so.

And all along she taught me stuff about books and how to spend money and how to dress.

She lowered the sunglasses and looked at me through the sliding glass door.

She puckered her lips and mimed "I love you, Jonny."

And I knew then, right then, that I'd been boning my mother.

Not this rich, slick woman with those fine long slender legs and the breasts like good sized coffee cups full of milk. Rebuilt. God. They were rebuilt. She was this rebuilt wreck of a woman whose wounds were hidden under layers of fake skin and whose legs wrapped around my waist trapping me in her mother mouth.

Just then, as I saw her face in the sunlight, her mouth forming love words, I saw her as a hag, someone I had to get away from and I wanted to puke. In the sunlight the scars were little white worms creeping from chin to eye socket, eye socket to earlobe, earlobe to neck. How many times had my fingers run over that skin? How many times had I seen that destruction without seeing it?

I left her reading Marquez' *Love in the Time of Cholera* again. She loved the book, all of Marquez. I walked to the bathroom and looked at myself in the mirror where I peered into the eyes of this boy who'd been dipping his dimple in his mama and I said, No. She owned everything in the room. Me. 26 years old. Sun-burned hair. Broke. Getting a little bit thick in the belly. Ugly. I hated what I saw. Everything I touched was hers. Nothing was mine. I had to get away. But it's hard to eat off a paper plate when you've gotten used to crystal and silver. Somehow steak tastes better when you slice it with a real silver blade. Wine tastes better when you sip it out of a crystal goblet. Caviar tastes better when it's served on bone china.

I had given in because I wanted her to love me.

I wanted all the little things she had done for me.

No, you don't look good in gabardine, Jonny.

You look splendid in yellow and black.

Those Italian shoes make your feet look sleek as a cheetah.

Come here, let me feel your muscles.

God, such shoulders. You're like a bull.

And at the table, showing me how to hold a fork, how to cut with a knife, how to pour wine so it didn't dribble, how to sip brandy.

Something had to give.

That afternoon, it all showed.

The scars, the stitches, the money it took to keep that body tanned and tight, it all showed.

I didn't want to touch her, ever.

I needed to get as far away as I could. And stay away.

But the silk sheets.

I looked the mirror and there she was.

Behind me.

She said, "Honey, what's the matter?"

I took a long deep breath.

"Nothing."

"Are you ill?" Her hand on my shoulder. I shuddered. "You disappeared." she whispered, mouth to my ear. "Jonny, did you find it?"

"Find what?"

"The toy? It's on the bed."

She nuzzled my neck. Her hands laced around my waist.

"Don't, Bea."

"Johnny. I need it. Right now."

I pulled loose, turned to face her, her mouth open and pleading the way it did when she was hot and wanted me to tie her up and use those toys she bought to make her scream, open her up, wide, get inside her until she came.

"No, Bea."

She backed away.

"Oh god," she said. "You hate me."

"I don't hate you."

"I need you, Jonny," she whispered again. "Come on. Now."

She grabbed my hand and pulled me toward the bed where the black harness lay spread out on the comforter.

She held it up.

"See? The buckles are stainless, please?"

"Bea, Stop. Just stop."

She stopped mid word, "Uh, Jon."

"Why did you tell Mel to fire me?"

"Why do you bring that up now? It's all over."

"No, it's not over."

"You want to know?"

"Yes."

"Because I'd been watching you, Jonny."

"What?"

"Since you went to work for Mel."

"Watching me?"

"Waiting for you. Waiting for the right time."

"For Christ's sake."

"I needed for you to notice me. How many times did I come in there and you ignored me?"

"You were a client. I saw your car."

"And you had all these sunshine honeys begging you to bed them down."

"It's not like that. I haven't touched anyone since I met you."

"What do you want, Jonny?"

"I want out."

"Out?"

"Out. I can't stay here anymore."

She slid up against me.

"No really. Tell me what you want, honey? I'll get it for you, baby. Just tell me what you want, sweetheart. Am I making it hard on you?"

"Bea, you don't know."

"I know you make me wet, Jonny. I know I make you hard, and I know I can come ten times when you take me."

"You don't get it. I'm leaving."

"You like nice things. You want nice things."

"I don't want anything," I said.

She shook her head. "You know, your accent comes back when you get mad."

"Bea."

"I've been good to you, Jonny. I gave you everything and the one time I want something, you do this to me. It's not fair."

She folded the leather harness with its chrome buckles and she stuffed it into the toy drawer with her cache of glass and black dildos and the steel chains and the bottle of cherry lube.

She walked to the door.

Turned. "You have hurt me, Jonny," she said.

"This time is different, Bea."

"How is this time so different?"

"I'm all messed up," I said.

"When were you not messed up, hon?"

"I see you in a different light."

"Light does strange things to people in LA."

"No, Bea. I saw you. I thought about my mother."

"Oh dear," she said. She came back to me. "Is that all? I'm not your mother. Do you want me to be your mother?"

"I don't know what I want."

"This is LA, Jonny. Money lets a woman be free enough to have a younger man. If you were older and I were young, would that be different?"

"I don't know," I said.

"Can I touch you, sweetheart? Please? Let me make it better. One touch. That's all. Just one touch. All right?"

How do you say No to your mother? I didn't say no.

Santa Monica Film School

After that, I quit reading her books.

I watched movies. Streamed them on the web, rented them from the video store down in the Village, ordered them from catalogs, got on mailing lists and joined video clubs. If Beatrice read books, I swam in movies. Old black and white movies, silent movies. *Picnic, Casablanca, Breakfast at Tiffany's.* Hundreds of movies. Five, six, seven a day. I ran my own film festival right in the den with the 54 inch TV and six cartridge DVD player so I didn't have to wait to start the next movie.

Movies are unsettling when you think about them. All these images filling you up. With what? Dreams.

I registered at the video store and I got mailings from film institutes inviting me to become a screenwriter, dream writer, dreams, lots of dreams in the movies and everyone in LA is a dreamer. I got flyers about script writing programs for the computer: "Your screenplay practically writes itself with our program," the promos said. Somewhere in there, the lie got hold of me. Bit me. Infected me with the dream sickness—write a script, make a mint, break away from Beatrice. Oscar. Best Screenplay.

I had a plan for working my way clear and so one night I told Bea I wanted to go to film school. That was a mistake. She broke down.

So I took her head-on and told her I was moving out.

"Where will you go, honey?" she asked me.

"I've gotta change," I said.

"But why? It's perfect the way it is."

She gave me everything except what I needed. How do you tell a woman you don't love her but you'll wet your wick in her? How do you tell her you'll spend her money, you'll drive her cars and sleep in her bed, but god damn it, you won't love her?

"What do you need, Jonny?"

"We've been over this before," I said.

She was crying. The first time I saw her cry was that night. Pitch black LA rainy night, the whine of wind in wires and eucalyptus trees and Beatrice wailing at me, mooncalf tears. Broken.

"I need to get control of my life," I said.

"What do you want that I can't buy for you?"

"Self-respect."

"Oh god. Not that?"

She collapsed. Just sort of gave out at the knees, her body melted, bones turned to jelly, and she's on the floor a pile of skin and tears and then I see she's pissed herself like she's dead.

"For Christ's sake, Bea." I picked her up. Stripped off her robe and took her to the bathroom.

A bird. Christ, she's so light, bird light, easy. The first time I ever picked her up, flaccid.

Flaccid. A big word. A Beatrice Building a Bigger Vocabulary word.

I could drop her. Walk out. Leave her on the floor. But she grasped my hand and kissed at me, a dying woman gasping for air.

So I washed the stink off her. Used a clean white soft monogrammed washcloth laced with the cinnamon smell of her personal soap, and she quivered as my hands glided over her body, between her legs, over her breasts.

"Jonny, you don't have to love me," she whispered.

I dried her off with one of the big beach-sized white towels. On my knees. Looking up at her. Her mouth quaking.

"I feel like you've got me in a prison here, Bea."

I wrapped her in the white towel, carried her to bed. Sat her on the edge of the bed while I pulled back the duvet and fluffed the pillows filled with goose-down. She let the towel slide off her. I laid her in, tucked the duvet around her.

"Then I have to die," she said, "I'll slit my wrists."

And she tried to sit up, fingernails gouging at me when I held her back.

I shoved her on the bed, raptor talons slicing at my hands, and locked her arms to her sides strait-jacket tight and sat on her.

"You're not doing anything stupid," I said.

Tears.

Whimpering.

The whimpering reminded me of a golden retriever pup I whacked once with a switch after it ran into the street. It whimpered and piddled on the floor.

Silence.

Hours of silence.

In the morning I've still got her pinned down. Groggy. The bed stinks of piss. Even rich women make a bed stink when they piss it.

I let her up. She's prim now. Ashamed of her nakedness.

"Why didn't you wake me up?" I ask.

"I didn't want to disturb you."

"Are you feeling okay?"

"I'm filthy," she says. Maybe she even blushes. "Am I naughty?"

Still have her under suicide watch.

I scrub her down in the shower, shampoo her hair with lemon. She pulls me into the steam, kisses me and then she's on her knees and she's sucking my cock, water running over us and then we're standing up against the wall and she comes apart like a train wreck, her hands tear at me, carve big chunks of meat out of my back, cannibal sized chunks and we fall out of the shower and keep going on the countertop until she's exhausted and my cock is bloody.

And she needs to be held.

So I hold her.

We lie on the pool deck, in the sun, naked.

Later when she can let go, we inspect the bed for damage.

The gray duvet is worthless. The feathers matted, the cover streaked with sweat and piss and spit.

She calls a junk man who hauls away the pissed-in-bed and then we shop. Buy everything—king-size bed, easy chairs, dressers, mirror, carpet, drapes until the bedroom is new. No more piss, no more death wish.

All fixed up she pretends nothing has changed.

She's contrite.

I start in again.

"I want to write," I tell her.

She smiles. "You can be good," she says. "A novelist."

"No! No novels," I say. "I'm gonna go to film school. I'm gonna be a screenwriter."

"You don't know what you're getting into."

"It's what I want."

"It's what you think you want."

"How do you know what I think?"

"All right. All right. You'll need money."

"I'll go back to work."

"As a mechanic?"

"As a mechanic," I said.

"Look at you. You can't live on twenty dollars an hour now." She laughs at money. Twenty dollars to her is nothing. She doesn't count her money. She weighs it. "Listen to me, my love. I know about these things. I know artists and writers. I can help you."

"God damn it, Bea, I want this to be me!"

"How much does it take to go there? To this film place?"

"I'll sell my car. It's good for ten or fifteen grand."

"Sell your car. Oh dear. Are you upset with me, Jonny?"

Shit.

She had three languages. When she was reading and talking about books—brain language. When she was having sex—primal grunt language. The third one was for everything else.

Brain language, I now understood.

Sex language, I was good at.

But the third was a foreign language. Nothing in it made sense. She went from buying me to trying to kill herself and pissing in her bed, to total innocence. *Do what you want, Jonny. You'll need money, Jonny. Are you upset with me, Jonny?* The next day I make the move to change my life.

It's a rainy, grainy, gray LA day. I leave Bea reading in the library.

She shrugs when I tell her I'm taking the Jag, that I'll be late.

A Man Walking By

PCH stinks of engine oil and diesel and kelp filtered through bleu cheese. Traffic stops. Accidents. Fires. Helicopters. Even the leather in the Jag smells bad. An omen.

The first thing you notice about the Santa Monica Film School is that it's a place where writers go to die. They don't give a damn if you bleed to death on the sidewalk in front of the place, a hundred other wanna-bes will file in over your dead body. Four openings for the next class, first come, first served, no favorites, everybody knows somebody so go to hell if you don't get the paperwork in right now.

I get enrollment papers. Fill them out over a cup of coffee.

They don't want a college degree, they don't care if you have a high school diploma, they don't care if you're an illiterate Okie, but they do want your money.

For a year-long course.

A lot of money.

More than I have even if I sell the Ford and go back to work and land a new career robbing tourists at Disneyland.

I have to make a choice. Sell the Ford—still won't cut it. Let Bea buy a new world for me the way she buys me clothes?

You look so handsome in blue, Jonny. And yellow is such a sunny color on you. You look good for such a bad boy. Come here.

I don't like blue.

Maybe I can work out a loan or something. Yeah. Right. With Bea. A loan.

When I get back to Palos Verdes Estates it's still drizzling that sweaty kind of LA drizzle that falls for a couple of days after a storm like someone forgot to turn off the spigot all the way.

I run the Jag into its slot in the garage. And there's plenty of room because the Ford is gone from its space against the wall. I'd been gone four hours.

Bea is still in the library.

"Where's my Ford?" I ask her.

"I gave it away," she says.

Stunned. "What?"

"To a man who was walking down the street."

"You slut," I say, "You...you slut."

"Well, it's gone, honey, and your filthy mouth won't bring it back."

"You gave it away?"

"To tell the truth I paid him to drive it off. Fords don't belong in Palos Verdes Estates. Just knowing it was in our garage made me ashamed. You're happier in the BMW aren't you?"

"You paid him?"

"I'm sure there's an article in the covenant about Fords. How do I look when you're the only one in a Ford?"

She closes her book, "Queer" by William Burroughs. Hands me an envelope.

"Money. He actually paid for it," she says. "For your car. So you can go to your precious film institute."

A man becomes his car when he rebuilds it. Women get nipped and tucked, they go to spas for mud baths and manicures to be made over. A man rebuilds and repaints and remakes his car from the axles up and he is the car and the car is him and when it's done right it's "My Fair Lady" on Michelins.

When somebody takes that from you, you have nothing. You're stripped down to bone and blood. There's no meat left on you. You live in a house, but your car is you.

I knew the money in the envelope was hers. She just gave me twenty grand.

Make a new life.

Become an artist.

Okay. I'll spend it. Twenty grand breaks down to about ten bucks a pop. I'm a ten dollar whore but I've got self-respect.

Uncertainty

I'm uncertain now. Used to be I had a stranglehold on reality. Knew what to expect, what to eat, what to wear, what to buy. But the last four years loosened that grip. Bea is hard.

I got soft eating her food, spending her money, driving her car, slipping it to her for ten bucks a shot. Used to be I paid for it—no consequences that way. Slam down a hundred bucks on a dresser somewhere, get your blow job and her out of the car, sometimes didn't even unbuckle.

But now…

It's like there's this show called "Sex with Bea" and it's a long German opera, takes three days just to figure out who the characters are.

Bea does that.

Money does that.

Being me does that.

There's no way out, no redemption.

The Problem is Love

I didn't enroll in film school looking for love. I was looking for a way out from under Bea's mothering. I was ashamed of what I'd let her do to me and who I was and what I was so I went looking for a way out. I figured I'd do what everyone else in LA was doing—write a screenplay. Get rich. Make my mark. Pick up my Oscar. Buy a Ferrari. Sleep in satin sheets.

Before Beatrice, I was a mechanic earning 22 bucks an hour.

She was my ticket out of Mel's Body Shop. A ticket with a nice mouth and a tan and money. You never see past those things until it's too late and by then your soul is shriveled and you're no good anymore.

So I guess I went to the film school looking for a way to put some yeast back into my soul—to make it plump up. Like a loaf of bread.

I didn't know why Vivian was there. What can you ever know about women? Later I see she's blocked. She's got a story, a draft, but she can't finish the rewrite. Later I see that's the way she is. Later I see she can't take anything all the way to the end.

It doesn't matter. You fall and after the fall nothing matters.

She was just a little thing who slipped in late the first night and blinked green flaring eyes at me.

Something broke off inside me. A chunk of my heart? My lungs? She owned me.

Shoulder-length curly black hair splashed with highlights in the neon.

It was like a 50-car California Speedway smashup inside my head.

Sat in a corner by the door. Exotic-looking. Ankle-length white dress.

Didn't hear what Mackey, the instructor, was saying for half an hour.

Smooth muscular arms. Small hands. Long unpolished nails.

She caught me staring at her and I fell into her eyes. Way down. For keeps.

She smiled. White dangerous teeth. Lips the color of coral.

Something opened up that had never opened before. With Beatrice, the only thing that opens up is her checkbook and I hate myself when I dip into the cash.

I guess the thing is—Vivian was a way to stop hating myself. I never have minded mounting a woman who needed it and wanted it and Beatrice was desperate for it so there was some satisfaction knowing I had what she wanted. When I met Vivian, I'd been in Beatrice's bed for four years. I'm not the boy I was four years ago. The grease is gone from under my fingernails and I wear a little bit of gold around my neck but I still taste black strap molasses and pinto beans and I hate myself when I look in the mirror.

Vivian's look.

I don't think Vivian expected it either. She smiled and that was it—we're in the hallway talking like I've known her forever. Like I said, you always remember the beginning and if it's good you always remember the ending. When I look back, I see that my world ended the night when she crossed her legs and looked at me and smiled.

"What's your story about?" she asked me.

"It's about a mechanic."

"So you write about cars?"

"You write what you know," I said.

You're never ready for love when it comes like a storm of African bees in your brain.

Vivian made me an expert on love. Pain does that to you—makes you dig under the scab to poke at the truth of pus. Until Vivian I'd never been in love. No one loves a little Okie boy from Turlock who carries the smell of cold piss to school on his jeans—"You pee your pants, Jonny?" They taunted me until I got big enough to knock heads together.

Now I'm an expert. A love machine. And I'm writing about it. For Mackey. To write a script. To win an Oscar...

Beatrice had taken an Okie mechanic and built herself a personalized sex machine. Later, after it's all over but the shouting, I see that I loved the wrong woman. Beatrice loved me enough to kill something for me. *Do you love me?* Nobody says it has to be reciprocal.

Reciprocal. A big word. She had gotten me looking at words. I gouged words out of Building a Better Vocabulary 'cause I thought—big mistake—a writer needs a lot of words and the words have to be big words. Then I found out screenwriters need just the basic three hundred. The grunt words. Sweat. Smash. Grind.

This was the difference with Vivian. Vivian in white only needed half a dozen, a dozen at the most, to say everything that was important to the whole human race.

Beatrice in black loved me. Will love me. Nothing changes there. Only now I see. *Do you love me?*

Tuesday nights became holy days for me. Thursdays were Xmas and my birthday all at once. Looking at Vivian I felt alive and real and I felt like I could do anything, anything at all. I guess it was that yeasty feeling of getting pumped up again, of being full that kept me coming back.

We talked about our work during breaks. There's no one else around. I mean people are there, but who gives a shit? I didn't have a draft of anything and Vivian was already into a rewrite. She asked me if I would read it.

I was in love and would have licked the menstrual blood off her thighs. I'd have done anything for her and I wouldn't have hated myself when I looked in the mirror afterward. That's purity.

So I read it.

Took an afternoon by the pool after I'd worked on Beatrice's scream for an hour or two—I lose time when I'm hanging by my thumbs—and then she went out. That's how low we had gotten in our relationship—she doesn't leave me alone unless she'd milked me dry. It's like she can feel me stretch the tether. There's more than one way to keep a man locked up.

Vivian's script was about a woman penned in a loveless sexless hopeless marriage to a Mafia don. I hoped it wasn't autobiographical.

When I finished reading it, I was even more in love. Trembling. Hungry. Kind of anxious and weird.

She needed me.

She didn't know anything about me but she needed me.

When I handed her the script on Thursday night she hugged it to her chest. All day I'd smelled her on the pages. I asked her what the scent was. She said it was <u>Secret</u>. She'd dabbed a drop on the pages just at the top where you turn and so her smell was on me. Deep in me. And that was good.

"Did you like it?"

"Judith's got a problem."

"Is it a script?"

"I don't know what a script is," I said.

"You didn't like it."

"I didn't say I didn't like it."

"But there's something wrong with it."

"I don't know that there's anything wrong with it."

"You're a mechanic. Can you fix it?"

"I don't have the right tools for that. That's why I'm here."

She looked at me. We didn't have to say it. It was there. Nothing else mattered then. Thursday night we cut our first class.

Afterwards, it's the first thing I write for Mackey. It spills all over the page.

```
LONG SHOT AS A BLACK MERCEDES
CRUISES UP PACIFIC COAST HIWAY.
NIGHT

INT. MERCEDES. NIGHT

ON a woman wearing a green
dress. Short. Tennis player
thighs glisten in the dash
light.

The driver's hand caresses her
thigh.

              WOMAN
```

```
          Slow down.

     She points.

               WOMAN
          Here. It's right here.

     ON a sign—MALIBU INN.

     MERCEDES running up a driveway.

     INT. MALIBU INN ROOM. NIGHT

     Tight shot of man and woman
     kissing.

     ON her face over his shoulder
     as she whispers:

               WOMAN
          I've never done this
          before.
```

Tuesday she's not in class. My heart goes into fib. Guy Mackey, the instructor—eight scripts in the can, two novels, a dozen articles on writing—is preaching about subplot. I know all about subplot now but god damn it, the problem is when she's not there I can't get any plot down. Mackey gets deeper into subplot and I understand that for the first time in my life I feel a need for someone. I need her, Vivian, 'cause I know I'll never be able to write if she isn't there with me. That smell. Secret.

I'm dead.

Do I call her?

Drop by her house?

One night at the Malibu Inn and she drops me. Drops the class.

So like a lovesick calf I go to her house. Bawl at her window. Munch her lawn.

She lives up Santa Monica Canyon. Half a mile up a winding eucalyptus-lined road. Lassen Drive.

The house is a '30s Craftsman.

I knock. A Latina answers the door.

"Señora isn't in," she says.

I go back to Palos Verdes Estates. To Bea. To the pool. She's on the deck wearing her black bikini, hair up in a black turban, heavy shades, mouth tainted crimson.

She looks at me.

"Where have you been?"

"Out."

"I don't like it when you go without telling me. At least a note. What if something happens?"

"What can happen?"

"I'm just thinking of you."

"You always think of me, Bea."

"There's a surprise on the bed," she says. She pulls her shades down, looks at me, smiles. I know what's next. Will it be a chain? A whip? A purple dildo? A vibrating butt plug?

Thursday night Vivian is back. Wearing yellow. Her hair down to her shoulders. The room lights up.

At break I corner her, "I came to see you."

"I know."

"You were home."

"I've never been with anyone but my husband."

"You feel guilty?"

"Yes."

She looked away. Shuffled her feet. I laughed.

'You think I'm going to make you pay for your sins?"

"You mean tell my husband?"

"Not me. I'll deny everything," I say. She touches my face. Cool fingers. Secret.

"You can teach me how to be unfaithful," she says.

Tuesday we cut class, run up to Ojai in her Mercedes. In bed at the Ojai Inn, I tell Vivian about the week in Cabo. About Beatrice's rent check to buy me out of my apartment.

"So it started out like a John O'Hara novel," she says.

"Sort of."

"You don't have to stay with her."

"I can't leave."

"Do you want to?"

"Look, there's a ton of shit hanging over me that I can't explain."

"She owns you."

"She's good for me."

"Tell me." She sits on the bed on her knees straddling me and slaps my cheeks. "Tell me or you won't get any more of what you like." Voice at a whisper. "Tell me. If you can't tell me, who can you tell?"

"This woman. She's got everything I never had. Everything I ever dreamed people could get. Some stuff I never dreamed people want."

"Does she give you what you want?"

"I don't want to go back to sleeping on a cotton mattress."

I tell her about Uncle Big. 600 pounds of gambling man with smooth delicate lotion commercial hands who made his living playing poker and how I slept on a piss-soaked cotton mattress in his trailer while my mother hustled drinks in the honky-tonk and brought Mexican laborers home and booted them out in the morning after I woke up. I tell her about breakfast of cold corn bread and molasses and a mouthful of pinto beans before I went to school. And I tell her about eyeing my mother asleep in bed her chestnut hair strung out on a pillow, her underwear piled on the floor and a cowboy snoring.

"I never knew people ate cornflakes for breakfast until I was twelve," I tell her. "I went straight from baby formula to pork chops and pork belly and beans. This is hard. Telling you. I can't leave her. I don't want to be poor."

"You are poor," she says. "You live in her life, in her house, sleep in her bed, swim in her pool. You need to break out on your own."

"And do what?"

"You can fix cars. You're good with cars and you have beautiful eyes."

"Beautiful eyes?"

"They're aquamarine. I don't know any woman who can resist that color."

"I don't want to be a crap-dollar-an-hour mechanic for the rest of my life taking bullshit from the Mels of the world."

"She wants you for your eyes. Any woman would die to have your eyes pillage her when she's dressing after you've had her."

"So that's how I trapped you?"

"No. It's all those muscles. I've always fantasized about sleeping with a truck driver. Just don't get carried away and break me."

Much later I tell Vivian about the day I left Turlock and rode over the Grapevine to the sea.

Thursday night in class I avoid Vivian. I sit across the room beside a cherry blonde who's writing her autobiography as a film script. I don't tell her it won't sell because nothing has happened to her to make anyone want to read about her life. My story, on the other hand, has pith and sex and adultery and sin and fornication and prevarication—now that's a story.

Vivian is cold at break. She tells me she doesn't like being snubbed. I tell her I'm not snubbing her. She wants to know what she's done to piss me off. I tell her she didn't do anything.

"I didn't know how you'd feel after my confession."

"I don't care where you came from and I don't care what you do. I love you and I love your eyes. But you can't have both of us."

"Why not?"

"That's not the way it works."

"Why didn't someone tell me this before?" I ask her.

"Because this is LA and you've got to find out shit for yourself."

Poison

I am poison. I am Death. She's alive if I don't touch her that first Thursday night in the hallway. It takes six months for the poison to work and I'm the spider who fills her blood with venom.

Wednesdays we rent a room at the Hotel Commodore on Santa Monica Boulevard. At first it feels like a foreign country to me. But Vivian—breathing Mother Earth— puts me at ease.

The room, our room faces the back on the fifth floor so you don't see the beach. You don't hear traffic or the chatter of tourists.

She likes it quiet. After we make love, she cries. Big, slow tears that frame her lips. I love that taste of salt and lipstick and her body on her own mouth. After the tears, silence. When I touch her now I feel beneath the skin to the blood, to the bone, down to the thing that makes her different from Beatrice, different from any woman I've ever touched.

"Peter's making me to go to Santa Barbara next week for five days."

"Say something came up."

"I can't."

"You can't why?"

"Clients. He has clients up there. I have to go and be the wife and I don't want to because I don't want to be with him, ever."

"Then don't go."

"He's turning mean on me."

"Tell me all of it."

"He forced me to have sex with him again."

She turns to face me. Small naked breasts with burnt umber nipples—like a doll. Her hair today is shattered by the reddish afternoon light bursting through the high window—a streak of red against the white pillow, white sheet.

"I was in my period. He didn't know I had a tampax in."

"How can he not know that?"

Her skin is warm, lustrous, smooth. I stroke her back, feel the angel wings of her scapula, the muscles of her back defined by years of playing tennis. I feel her skin, but I am her blood, I am the oxygen in her body, the salt in her tears, she naps naked nuzzled into my shoulder.

It is late. I smell the sea as it washes in the tide. I tug her loose from the sweat of the bond, kiss her mouth, get up. Naked. Dress.

"I have to go," I whisper letting the words lap at her skin like a liquid tongue. "I love you."

"You're a good teacher," she says.

"What?"

"I think I'm getting the hang of being unfaithful."

She stays. I leave. Outside I feel eyes for the first time.

I never hear the shutter click but I feel it. Look around. No one I know in a clot of sun-hungry tourists, but I feel the glass eye on me. I am found out.

Or is it just guilt?

When I get back Beatrice isn't in.

I shower. Check my body for marks, the remains of Vivian's fire. Today I get away clean. Tomorrow? Who knows? I try to imagine sex with a woman who's bleeding, who has a tampax in. I can't imagine it. Did she tell him? Did she? A man rapes his wife.

I have to act soon. Or lose her. I know that.

The house, mausoleum dark, very LA dark, a haunting dark, has its own perilous shadows and its own memory and its own hidden angers. The quiet and the smell and the feel of breath down my neck. Someone snapping photographs.

It's funny. I don't know where Beatrice goes when she leaves. She never tells me. I don't ask. I don't want to know. Do I care?

Where am I going? What am I doing?

Wednesday night, I think about Vivian while Beatrice screams, ankles chained together. I'd know if she had a tampax in. I'd know. But Beatrice doesn't need tampax. She's had her plumbing fixed, her phrase, *plumbing*. "You never have to worry, Jonny," she whispered the first time. Like I would worry. Maybe all the way to the bank.

So I write about killing him.

```
EXT. LASSEN DRIVE. DAY

Jonny parks the Jaguar on the
street.

        JONNY (V.O.)
     It was one of those May
     days in Los Angeles when
     you think you're in the
     tropics.

Jonny walks across a thick
lawn. Shush of sprinklers.

        JONNY (V.O.)
     I left the Jag on the
     street. I didn't want it
     crossbreeding with the
```

thoroughbreds Greg Fox
stabled on his estate.

Opens gate that leads down to
the swimming pool.

> JONNY (V.O.)
> Greg Fox had made it
> big. The right house,
> beautiful wife,
> teenage daughter
> pried from the
> Southern California
> Beach Goddess mold.

Soundtrack from *Diva*.

> JONNY (V.O.)
> Greg was pulling down
> 2 Mill a year, easy.
> A man could live on
> that. I envied him,
> but not enough to
> kill him.

Greg Fox lies on his belly in a
pool of blood.

The back of his head caved in.

A Wheaten Terrier beside him.

> JONNY (V.O.)
> He lay beside his
> pool looking like the
> god of water. I felt
> sorry for the dog,
> and I felt sorry for
> myself. I knew that
> Fox had been dead for

```
less than thirty
minutes because I had
just been talking to
him on the phone.

Jonny kneels beside the bodies.

        JONNY (V.O.)

This put me in a bad
position. If there
was anyone who didn't
need Greg Fox dead it
was me. I was
sleeping with his
wife.
```

After I write it, I tear it up. Burn it. Write it again. I have to show Mackey something soon. "You need some pages," he says, "you all need some pages, so god damn it, let's see some pages."

All right Mackey. I'll give you pages.

All day Thursday I scribble words on yellow pages. I've bought a script writing program for the computer but if I use it I just sit and stare at the colored screen. If I write by hand, I can erase, scratch out, fill the pages with nothing and it still looks like a man hard at work. I write a love scene. I realize that all I'm doing is writing about Vivian. I regret burning the scene with Peter dead beside the swimming pool. I will never finish anything. Maybe I'm not destined to finish.

Thursday evening, on the deck, I study the jacaranda, the agapanthus in its blue grace, the palm trees, the hungry peacocks who perch on the roof pitch watching me. I have read about birds. How feathers evolved. How birds only breed when their body fat is high. How sometimes you can't tell a male from a female until you examine the sex organs. Imagine. Vivian. Bea.

I'm digging a hole and falling in it.

I have to make a decision.

Soon.

Before I'm too old.

Vivian tells me she's not a can of peaches I put on a shelf and take down when I want some sugar. She's ready to leave Peter. *"But I'm afraid," she says. "There's too much history. My god, I mean we have every Thanksgiving and every Christmas at our house and I play tennis with his mother."*

The garage door buzzes open. My gut tightens up. The 850 rumbles in. The peacocks abandon me for her. They know her sounds. They call for the sound of the feed bin opening. I hear her cluck for them. The birds flutter.

The sky turns a deeper sunset red.

Beatrice closes the door. She's quiet.

She comes out to the deck holding the mail.

"You didn't pick it up," she says.

"Where have you been?"

"Out. Jonny?" She sits splay-kneed across from me in a deck chair the way Uncle Big used to sit when he wanted to have a man-to-man chat.

"What?"

"Do you love me? Even a little bit?"

"I'm here."

"No you're not. You're not here anymore. You're off somewhere... I..."

"What?"

"Nothing. It's not enough just to be here. You have to be here."

"I'm right here."

"I want you to stop pretending you love me."

"I can't figure you out."

"You get what you want and then I don't matter," she says.

She lets out a big sigh. Sits back in the deck chair. Reads the mail.

I'm in the kitchen when she nuzzles up to my back.

"Mmmm. You smell fresh," she says. "Like after a rain. Jonny stay with me tonight."

"It's Thursday. I've got pages to turn in."

"Let's have lobster at Clio's."

"I'll get a sandwich on the way."

She lets me go.

I look at her.

She looks beaten, hurt. Usually, now, I'd think about the gold Rolex and the closet full of clothes and I'd get my panic feeling and I'd slam her onto her knees dog-love till she's panting and begging me to let her come. But not on Thursday nights. Not now.

"What's happening to you, Jonny?" she says as I walk out the door.

In the Jaguar, I discover that I've forgotten my pack with the pitiful pages I've gotten down after eight weeks of writing for Mackey.

I go back in. Beatrice is still in the kitchen pouring a glass of white wine. Very good wine.

Her face brightens. She looks better now than she did just a minute before. Tense. Her legs tight. But the black skirt makes her look mournful.

"I forgot my pack."

Her face clouds. She licks the rim of the wine glass. "I love you," she whimpers.

Thursday nights are sacred. Writing. Class. Vivian. My story is a sham. I'm no better than the autobiographical blonde who sits against the wall. I don't have a story. I lay my pages on Mackey's desk. Watch them bleed stupidity, ugly, insipid. I hate my writing. I hate myself for pretending to be a writer.

I go to class just to see Vivian, to breathe her air, hoping for a secret grope in the hall. I can't get enough of her body. One day a week can't feed me enough of her mouth. When I look at her, my eyes feel full, powerful. My skin feels alive, my mouth feels real, my brain feels like a powerful engine revving high and smooth. And I want more of her. I want her all the time.

Tonight Vivian dresses in black. First time I've seen her in black. I get antsy. Too much like Bea. Black. In black *she* looks like an angel.

"We have to talk," she says.

"Okay."

Guy Mackey wants us to learn about splat. Splat is what happens when your character runs out of gas, hits imaginary walls, when your character fails miserably before getting what she wants. Splat.

At break I trap Vivian against a wall. She's flushed red. Nervous.

"We're in trouble," she says.

"You're pregnant."

"I wish I were. I told him."

"What did you tell him?"

"That I haven't been faithful to him."

"When?"

"Tonight. An hour ago."

"What did he say?"

"Nothing, but he'll pretend I never said it and we'll go away for the weekend and while we're away he'll want to have sex and I can't stand to have him touch me anymore and so he'll get hurt and he'll shut me out and when we come back it will be like it never happened because he doesn't have an inner life and he can't imagine me with anyone else so he doesn't want to know as long as I stay with him."

"Are you going to stay with him?"

"I've never done this before," she says.

It's probably true. The first night we made love at the Malibu Inn she didn't ask me if I had protection. She didn't know how to be naked with a stranger. When I touched her, she trembled. Skin on skin. Not a word about AIDS or STDs or anything. We were Adam and Eve, the first virgins doing something that had never been done before. That first night, with her, I came for the first time—virgin all over again, both of us. When you get that, you have everything.

The whole situation's heavying up now, too heavy and pretty soon it'll spill on the floor. All messy.

"Would he put a detective on you? Have you followed?" I ask her.

"He doesn't *want* to know anything," she says.

"I was photographed outside the hotel."

"Oh god."

"It's not Peter?" I say.

"Oh no."

It's clear to both of us. She touches my cheek. She's not afraid to touch me now, around other people, leaning against the wall. I need to make love to her, find an empty room and make love to her standing up.

"What do you mean you wish you were pregnant?"

"You heard me."

"Vivian, what do you mean?"

"Stupid," she says. "You're a stupid slug."

My Name is Jonny Wattron

I can't sleep. I feel Beatrice—a heavy weight. I go to the same bed with her, night after night, feel that weight of her body, her sweat. She sleeps innocent. Her dreams are quiet. I leave her, go sit by the pool to watch the sun come up over the San Gabriels. It's blood red, stained, reminds me of Lorca's *Bodas de Sangre*—the same color as Vivian's Chinese silk robe with the embroidered gold dragon that wraps around her body.

Since Vivian and I started there have been a string of special moments. I was a poor man but now I am rich because I've stolen time and found forever in her eyes.

"You are the first, last, and only thing I have loved in this world. I'll have to pay because a man like me doesn't deserve that kind of love."

Vivian is right. I have to choose.

I remember the day I brought Vivian to the house on Via Campesina. I knew it was a mistake because once I had slept with her in Beatrice's bed, that was all I saw—Vivian.

Beatrice was off at a class reunion. They chartered a ship to San Francisco, flying back. Four days of Vivian and me in the house and it was like we were married. Seeing her on the deck in her white suit, naked if I asked her to swim naked, sex in the pool if I asked her to, barefoot on the hot concrete deck, her sunglasses pushed up on her forehead, a trickle of sweat on her nose as she came holding on to me as though I were the last and only lover she could ever have. I knew then I didn't deserve her. I knew it because a boy from Turlock whose Uncle Big was a gambler, a boy from Turlock whose mama went down for cowboys in a trailer while the boy slept in his jeans and T-shirt, that boy didn't deserve an angel.

I told her about Beatrice's husband. Told her about his testicular cancer. How they castrated him. How he brought home whores to make movies while he shot heroin and watched them, begging Beatrice to join in. How Beatrice slept alone after that, feeling the weight of his body still against her, feeling sorry for him because his sex was so perverse—what choice does a man have when his testicles have been cut off?

The last day Vivian slept in Beatrice's bed she laid down the law.

Cross-legged on the bed, naked, her hair still sweat-wet from coming, she said, "I have to do something about Peter. I can't stand being in the same house with him. His father died."

"I love you. When I look at you, I feel you in my eyes like fresh water."

"Did you hear me?" Vivian combed at her tangled hair.

"His father died. I can't just walk out of there."

She grabbed me by the shoulders and shook me.

"If you keep putting it off, you'll lose both of us. You think she doesn't know?"

"She doesn't know anything."

"You think you're so smart." She let me go.

"Do you love me?"

"Give me a reason I should love you."

First Time in the Loft

Like a dog, I guess you have to mark your place when you're slipping it to a married woman. Some animal something I didn't understand made me want to mount her in her own house, in her own bed. Pee in the Man's toilet. Poke around in his closet. Try on his shirts.

From the window of the house on Lassen Drive, you see the ocean just off Santa Monica. It was the first time we'd been in her bed, the first time I'd been in her loft where she kept her computer and the drafts of her screenplay, the first time I'd seen her in her own space.

A woman in her own space is all new, every time. Outside, in the street, in the hotel, she is always a stranger, making amends, looking for a way to avoid conflict, but in her space, she's like a smooth walking gazelle so that even her nakedness seems new and intact and natural.

Vivian was so pure she squeaked.

"Is this where you and Peter make love? Made love?"

"No. This is my room. This is mine. I'm sorry."

"For what?"

"For making you suffer. That's the first time I've ever said that to a man in this room."

My throat locked up. Jesus. When I was with her, I felt like I was another man, a real man.

"I have money. Enough for everything you'd ever want."

"What are you saying?"

"Leave her. Let's go to Mexico. We can be there in six hours."

The words stopped me. She was soft as sunrise, rich as snowy mountains. She lay on her back, arms behind her head, offering but already spent, small breasts pouted at me.

"What are you telling me, Vivian?"

"We won't be poor."

"How? Peter?"

"Forget Peter. It's Marilyn I worry about."

"Marilyn is?"

"My mother. A widow."

"I didn't know that."

"I didn't want to scare you away."

I touched her, felt her melt under my fingers, wet, the first woman I'd ever made love to who ejaculated, came wet, and loved her wetness.

"We can start over in Mexico," she said. "Start over, wipe that woman out of your life. I want you to write, Jonny. You've got more talent than I'll ever have. I know that. You need to write. I know that when you're writing, you're alive. I want you to be alive."

"Just touching you makes me alive."

"Don't make fun of me."

"You think I'm making fun of you? Life and death, right?"

"Shit piss—god damn you. Why? Why when I'm not with you do I feel dead?"

He usually came home at 6:00 o'clock. I left her in her Chinese red robe, hair a mess—"I'll tell him I just got back from a run at the beach," she said.

I didn't leave right away. I sat in the Jaguar on Lassen Drive under the eucalyptus trees. I still smelled like Vivian. Her wetness had its special odor. I waited until he drove up. Watched him get out of his bullet gray Porsche. I studied his walk. A small man. Small as Vivian. He looked at me in the Jaguar, then went inside.

I was jealous. Till then, it had been abstract. He got her. He had her. I hated him. I wanted him dead.

When I got home, I rewrote the pool scene.

```
EXT. LASSEN DRIVE. DAY

Jonny opens the gate down to
the swimming pool.

          JONNY (V.O.)
     Greg Fox lay beside
     his pool looking like
     the god of water.

Soundtrack of Diva.

Greg Fox looks up at Jonny.

          GREG
     What do you want,
     asshole?

          JONNY
     You. Dead.

ON the dog, Baxter, a Wheaten
Terrier wagging his tail.

Jonny and Greg struggle. Jonny
plunges a knife into Greg's
neck. Greg drops into the pool.

Jonny stands holding the bloody
knife.

Greg's body floats face down in
the pool.
```

```
            JONNY
       That's for
       Vanna...Asshole.

Jonny tosses the knife into the
pool, stoops, washes his hands.

Pets the Wheaten Terrier.

EXT. LASSEN DRIVE. DAY

ON the Jaguar headed down to
PCH.
```

Then I burned it. I've burned everything I've worked up so far.

Vivian was wrong.

Writing doesn't make me feel alive. It makes me feel dead.

Capital City

The first time I go to church, I'm fourteen. Jane Beggs is Mormon, wants me to go to church with her. We take bread, water, she gives testimony.

That day I learn I'm damned to hell forever unless I repent, accept the Pearl of Great Price, jug Jane Beggs on Sunday afternoon in her front room on the floor while her parents are at church praying, drink the blood of Jesus and eat his flesh. If she gets pregnant, it's one more Latter Day Saint.

It gets to be a habit.

Then, I meet Beatrice. I remember all the other firsts—first time I drove a Ford over 110 MPH with Uncle Big in the passenger seat sweating, first time I came just looking at a Victoria's Secret model, first time Bea handed me a check for two grand—buy yourself something, she said.

Two grand.

Used to be I paid for sex, now I cash the checks, wash out my mouth with dollar bills, spend it on cologne and silk shirts I don't want or need. After you gas up and get new tires, what do you want money for?

That's my problem. Bea says I'm Okie white trash. It's true.

It changes when I meet Beatrice. Her house, her pool, her cars, her bed, her sheets, her checks, her food, me.

I'm another possession. I wear designer shorts but the hard on is still Okie white trash, the same hard on that came in Jane Beggs on Sunday afternoon after eating Jesus Christ and sucking his blood.

I'm deep into my own shame. I put the shame into scenes. Take the scenes to Mackey. Mackey reads the script, says it stinks like a three day toilet not been flushed after eating asparagus.

"How do I make it better?"

He's god, I'm a sinner. How do you repent? How do you atone? What is sin?

Am I a sinner for taking Bea's money? For writing her into a script? For screwing Vivian who's married? Am I a sinner?

You bet.

I used to hate sin, but now I just fold it up—use a silver money clip—and wallow in the news that I'm doomed to hell. It's enough to make a man join a church, but it's too late.

For me.

I'm bought.

Paid for.

Insured even.

Meeting Beatrice changes everything. I used to care, don't care now. Just ride her slippery, get off in the quick turns, then back on when she slows down.

Mackey says, "Bee is changing. She's becoming less maternal."

He sees something I don't. I'm grateful when God speaks to me.

"Your writing reminds me of corn whiskey," he says, "not smooth, just kicks the shit out of you till Monday morning, but it's not enough, Jonny, a man's gotta guzzle a little champagne with his strawberries."

Mackey is god. He pokes a finger at three words in my script and the whole thing turns to shit. And there's no redemption.

Bea wants to know where I go so early on Thursday night. I tell her. I meet with other writers. We read our work,

"Show me."

She doesn't trust me. I don't trust me. She is cautious. Hesitates to let me out of the house unless we've ridden the slippery train for an hour.

Then she cuts me loose.

Can't do much damage when your coal stoker's on strike, can you?

No god will have me, no church baptize me, no canon shrive me.

That leaves me nothing but Bea's whore, her sex-dog barking at her for a bone.

Maybe if I come with her enough times I'll pop through to the other side reborn as *pure* white trash.

Maybe I just haven't sinned enough to be worthy of redemption?

Maybe I'm a saint in disguise. A mechanic disguised as a screenwriter who uses words and images to make miracles where other saints used birds and bones.

Maybe I'm the Saint of Wanna-be Screenwriters.

Saint of the mixed metaphor.

Saint Rewrite.

I feel good.

I want to be clean and pure. I want to overcome my lapses, my transgressions. But I'm not ready to pay the price so I'll bathe in Bea's money and slide around on her silk sheets and come with her hanging upside down in the closet on meat hooks wrapped in plastic if that's what she wants.

I'm an angel of sin and sex.

God, I used to be such a good boy watching quietly from the shoe shine seats at the Royal Crown while Uncle Big raked in piles of green, his diamond flashing on his right pinky, a huge diamond that looked like a gnat's eye against his huge, fat, blubbery fingers.

I watched, pure and clean, wearing new jeans—never been washed—he bought me, and a new cotton T-shirt and new Nikes, and then I met Jane Beggs and I discovered sin.

Do you accept our Lord Jesus Christ as your savior?

I do, I do, now can we do it again?

Do you repent of your sins and drink the blood of Jesus?

I do, I do, now let me lie down between your legs.

Do you renounce all gods except the one true god, Jesus Christ, Prince of the Forever and do you take the flesh of Jesus Christ into your body to wipe away your sins?

I do, I do, now please let me taste your nipples, your thighs, I am only fourteen and I am addicted to your body, to your blood.

"You are damned, Jonny Wattron," Jane Beggs says, smiling, her mouth ruby red and pulsing and she is fifteen and full of figure and rich of limb and I feel, feel, feel the sins of Solomon and his Dark Love as I kiss her and I know that she is recruiting me for Mormon heaven, and I know now that I will cheat lie steal accept Jesus Christ if I can come in Jane Beggs one more time.

When I meet Beatrice I drop into the world of Real Shame.

It shows in the shiny paint of the Jaguar as I drive down PCH trolling for chicks in T-Birds. It shows in the silk shirts and the designer slacks and the leather interior of the BMW 850.

I am shameless in my shame, I am a saint of shame. And sin.

I am the patron saint of whoredom.

And I am a whore.

Vivian might be my salvation.

Bea might be my salvation.

If I can figure out what she wants.

I think she wants to kill me, but I'm not sure.

I had a friend whose balls bloated up as big as elephant's balls. "Got something from a girl," he said.

"Got what?"

"I don't know, but god damn I'm glad. She was something and I don't care if she's wrecked my life forever, I wouldn't trade that week for a ton of gold."

He was insane.

I am insane.

Bea is insane.

Vivian is insane.

We are all insane.

I'm the Patron Saint of Insanity.

I have to decide—do I want to be saved?

I have tasted the flesh of Jesus and it tastes like chicken.

I have drunk the blood of Jesus and it tastes like Chianti.

I have to get a grip on myself. Explore sin, go deep into it. Explore it like a scientist. Discover the seeds of transgression. Discover the sin in a mouthful of nipple, the truth in a hank of pubic hair.

I do want to be pure—pure sin—and I can achieve that with Bea's help.

She doesn't know.

Her money buys the toys of sin.

Her body accepts the root of sin the way a penitent's mouth accepts the wafer.

Together we discover Adam and Eve thirty times a week.

And each time we sink deeper into the dark. Lords of Xibalba.

Sin has no face, it does not age, it reveals itself like a small lamb in a wolf pack—innocent each time until the blood blossoms on the white, pure wool.

Blood.

I do have to get a grip on myself, slide deeper into degradation, dive all the way down then, maybe just then I'll be worthy of lamb's blood.

Until then, all I can do is hope.

Sin smells like Vivian's menstrual blood.

Sin tastes like Bea's cunt after an all nighter.

Sin feels like the slick gulf between Bea's legs.

Sin drives like an 850 CSi.

Sin is a big country and I am its capital city.

Sin is infinite I have decided—but there is only one way to be good and it doesn't taste like chicken.

I have been good and quite frankly I found it boring. Being thirteen.

Now I am a master of degradation. I am in love with sin.

Her mouth tastes like crushed pomegranate.

The Saint Francis

The trip to San Francisco was a mistake from the beginning. Too risky. But risk made it sweeter.

Beatrice wants to go see a friend on the Peninsula. I know we don't see her friends so I'll stay in the hotel—the Saint Francis—while she visits, rides, talks, drinks wine.

She hates to leave me alone now but she can't, won't show me to her friends. I'm her secret. The little man in the closet who makes her smile, who puts that glow in her cheeks.

She smells the betrayal on me.

The scent of another woman's sex drives her crazy but she says nothing.

Nothing turns into never letting me out of her sight.

Tuesday night, the night first draft is due, I tell Vivian about the trip.

"I'll miss four classes. What will Mackey say when I don't turn in a script?"

"What will I say?"

"Come with me."

"That's crazy."

But she thinks about it. Lies to her husband.

"One night only," she says.

Risk is an aphrodisiac—a Big Beatrice word—I know. All the way up the coast, through Carmel to San Francisco, I think about Vivian. I'm sick in love now. Thicker than blood.

I plot P's death. Write it six times. I don't write a word. I imagine it, get it in my head, can write it down anytime. It's a warm day in LA, the kind of sun-rich day that makes you forget the smog.

He dives into the pool. I hit him with the ax in one version.

Shoot him with a .38 in the next.

Cut his throat in the third.

Burn them all. Tear up the copy. Zap the file in Scriptwriter.

Want no evidence.

Beatrice insists on driving to the City. Drive, takes an entire day. Fly, we're there in a couple hours.

"I hate rentals," Bea says. "I like my own things."

It's a long day on the road but it's a good drive in the 850. Power. Class. A rich woman. The wrong woman, but a rich one.

"What are you thinking?" Bea asks me.

"How beautiful you are."

"Do you lie like that to all your women?"

"I don't have any other women."

"You better not. I'll kill them."

"Like a rat," I say.

"What?"

"I read that a female rat will kill other females in a cage to keep them from breeding."

"We're not in a cage," Bea says. "We're not breeders."

She knows. She knows. I don't care.

"Stay with me, Bea," her friend says when she calls from the Saint Francis.

"Can't," Bea says toying with the phone, watching me.

Can't show the Okie boy to her Peninsula friends. Can't live without him, can't live with him, what's a girl to do?

Always now, before she leaves me, we have sex. In the Saint Francis things are no different.

It's a powerful, animal rutting with no refinements just raw, courageous grunting until one of us falls asleep. It's an insurance policy on my gonads. Resilient gonads. Wonderful gonads.

She has no idea how good Vivian is for me.

Not any idea at all.

When I wake, Bea is gone. There is money on the bed, a lot of it, and a new Platinum Visa card in my name. There is a note. "Back later tonight. Be good. I love you. B."

I call the desk. Vivian is in room 1763.

An 18th Century room. 1763—Pre-Revolutionary.

"She's gone," I say. No answer, just the click of the connection breaking.

She wears green. An ankle length dress, deep dip at the neck to the tops of her sun-tanned breasts, a long slit up the side so when she walks her leg slices with provocative splendor.

It's a new world seeing her out of context, out of LA, out of the smog, out of class, out of the Commodore Hotel. Seeing her in a hotel room clothed.

"You smell like sex," she whispers as I peel the green dress from her shoulders.

I hold her, stroke her skin, supple, smooth, hot, sweaty.

"She sucks me dry before she lets me out of my cage," I tell her.

"She's smarter than you think," Vivian says.

"This is crazy. Bringing you all the way up here just to get into your pants."

"I'm not wearing pants," she says.

I can't keep her from filling my eyes. I'm at that place now—wanting to be in her, over her, around her, in her blood, in her lungs, smelling her sweat, between her legs touching her wetness until she comes on my fingers, and then licking them just to take into my body what has been in hers.

"This is all new to me," I tell her.

"What are you going to do?"

"What?"

"Some men take women to meet their mothers. You bring me to a hotel."

"It's a good hotel."

"I need an answer."

"Let's just take what we can get," I say.

"I've told Peter I want out."

"Oh god."

"He knows. He doesn't want to admit it."

"What do you want from me, Viv?"

"A decision. I can go either way here."

"Either way?"

"Either you leave her or you lose me."

"Why does it have to be either or?"

"Because I don't think you're man enough for the two of us." She laughs. "You're big, you're ugly, you smell bad. I don't know why I want you."

"It's the way I get in and out of the saddle."

She holds me off until we've stripped the sheets. She doesn't want to lie in Bea's sweat, roll in her sex. Her burning me for a decision cools as we heat up. There is sweeter sugar in forbidden fruit. The sweetest is being exactly where Be a had lain hours before.

The excitement surprises us both. This time it is different from every other time.

"I hate being the other woman," Vivian says, flushed with that peculiar redness at the throat—after-sex red, arousal-red, complete-red.

"You're the only woman who has ever lived. First thing I think of in the morning, last thing I think of at night."

"That's not enough, Jonny. I want to wake up with you in the morning, go to bed with you at night."

"Vivian."

"I don't want to share you."

In the next hour, I talk to her, use sex words to tell her how I want her, how I am using her, the words wash over her and she wants more.

The phone rings.

Bea.

"Okay," I say.

I look at Vivian in her bed, red throat like a robin now sitting up giving me the finger and baring her teeth at me. Makes faces.

Bea can smell her over the phone from fifty miles off.

"Dinner at Ernie's," I say. "I don't know where Ernie's is."

"Take a cab," Bea says.

I hang up.

"Jesus, why do I feel dirty?" Vivian says. "I can't do this anymore, Jonny, not like this. I'm not that kind of woman."

"What kind of a woman are you?"

"A settling down in a little apartment with a view of the ocean in Venice kind of woman. Make me happy, Jonny. What's so hard about that."

I smell poverty break out under my armpits. I smell it in the sweet scent of sex, the odor of pinto beans on my clothes, taste the dark heaviness of molasses, the crumbling cornbread.

"Let's just use the time we have," I say.

"And tonight, she walks in and gets into bed with you and I sleep alone."

"We're in the same hotel."

"I want to sleep in the same bed. Make a decision."

"Or what?"

"You don't know what I am, Jonny, or what I can do for you. You won't know until I'm gone and then you'll regret it."

"Is that an ultimatum?"

"I guess it is."

"Do you love me?"

"What?"

"Do you love me. Just say it."

"I'm going back to LA. Tonight. You won't change."

She dresses. I watch her sweet skin disappear under the green dress.

At the door, she looks back.

"I'll do it," I say.

"When?"

"When we get back to LA."

"Come with me right now," she says.

I hesitate.

She's at the door.

I have to decide. I can't decide. I've decided. Too much Beckett.

"Vivian. Tonight. At dinner."

"Yeah sure. I'll be in LA. Call me. or don't."

She's out the door. I am shot. The pain of seeing her gone is like a heart attack slamming me down.

I count the bills Beatrice left on the bed. A thousand dollars. A Platinum Visa card.

Room service sends a woman up to change the sheets and lay out fresh towels.

Dead Love

You look for the eyes, the hair. No longer in your fingers. Her face no longer in your eyes.

And you're alone.

After she walked out of that hotel room at the Saint Francis and said "Call me. Or don't", I was a changed man. Lost. Broken. Didn't know how bad the break was.

Dinner at Ernie's with Bea that night was pure pain with baked potato, a Caesar salad, and rosemary squab. I knew how the bird felt—decapitated, stuffed with wild rice.

Bea was lonely after her visit with her Peninsula friend. Vacant and empty as an abandoned lot—an existential mini-crisis that she filled with chocolate mousse and furtive toes raking my leg under the table.

"Why are you ashamed of me?" I asked her.

"I'm not ashamed of you."

"You don't let me meet your friends. You think I'll embarrass you with my Okie accent?"

"What is the matter with you?" Chocolate dot at the corner of her mouth. She touch it, suck the mousse from my finger.

"What's the matter with me is I feel like you don't want to be seen with me."

"And why is that?"

"Because people will think you're keeping me."

"I am keeping you," she said. "But that's not what's eating you." She leaned across the table, her foot kneading my crotch. "Tell Mama what's bothering little Jonny."

"You're drunk, Bea. I can't talk to you."

"Which is it?"

"What?"

"I'm drunk or you can't talk to me?"

"You're drunk. I can't talk to you when you're drunk."

Her foot dug deeper into my crotch. Toes like fingers playing arpeggios on my piano.

"Did you have a nice day, sweetheart?" she asked me.

"You mean did I spend the blood money you left on the bed?"

"Travel expenses. A boy shouldn't be without spending money in the big city."

"This isn't working, Bea."

"Only because you don't want it to work," she said.

"You are ashamed of me. When?"

She pulled her foot off my chair. Pushed away from the table, walked around to face me, lifted my hands and spread them square over her breasts. "Right here, Jonny, on this table, or take me back to the hotel and fuck me or do me in the car, I don't care."

"Bea. Come on."

"You think I'm ashamed of you? Embarrassed by you?"

"Bea, sit down."

"Jonny." She knelt. The Maître d' approached.

"Madame, is everything all right?"

"My lover thinks I'm ashamed of him and embarrassed by his accent."

"Does Madame need a taxi?"

"I'm going to suck his cock right here in your restaurant," she said.

I got up. She took my arm.

"I'm leaving, Bea."

I dropped money on the table. A hundred, two, hell, I didn't care. I just wanted to get out of there.

On the street she slapped my face. Crack. Stunned.

"Don't ever think you embarrass me, Jonny."

"Your Peninsula friend. You leave me here. Why don't I get to meet her?"

"Because she's an invert, Jonny."

"An invert?"

"A transsexual. She's a former boyfriend, Jonny, from Stanford days."

"Oh Christ."

"You can't embarrass me, honey, sweetheart." She groped me all the way back to the Saint Francis, all the way to LA, all the way. Insatiable.

I quit going to the Film Institute.

Settled into a black routine—movies, writing a little, sex, movies, writing, sex.

Bea was two women.

One of them suave, smooth, powerful, cosmopolitan.

The other a whimpering sex machine who turned to jelly when she came and never wanted to stop coming.

Opened up to Bea. Tried to get inside her. To use her fire to burn out the bleeding hematoma Vivian left on my heart, but the more I opened up to Bea, the bigger Vivian got.

Bea's eyes became Vivian's eyes sun-big, moon-bright.

Bea's sex-moans became Vivian's orgasmic screams.

And the more we were together, the bigger the hole in my heart became.

"I'm glad you gave up that stupid film place," Bea said.

Breakfast on the deck.

No more late nights alone. A married couple in bed at 11, up at 7. Breakfast together. Oatmeal. Eggs. Orange juice.

"It gave me up," I said.

"Oh sweetie, you can be anything you want to be."

"No I can't."

"You just have to want it really bad."

"No, Bea, there's something called talent and I only do things I'm good at so it looks like I never fail. But I don't have it."

"You're not a failure," she said. Hand on my hand.

"Anyone can make you come. Don't have to be an artist for that."

"I'm not that easy, Jonny."

"What do you mean by that?"

She looks at me, eyes wet, mouth wet.

"You make me wetter than I ever dreamed I could be. I don't know myself when I'm with you. You turn me into a river. It won't stop."

"It's not healthy to tell me that," I said.

"Why not?"

"What if I use it against you?"

"You mean hurt me? If you want to, hurt me."

"Shut up, Bea."

"I mean it. Anything."

"I'm not gonna hurt you."

Her black robe opens under the glass table top. Her bare legs show. She shivers.

When you first find the emptiness it doesn't scare you. You wake up and you're empty—maybe you're hungry, maybe you're thirsty, but then you eat and you're still not full. You know it's deeper than bananas or oranges, deeper than Cheerios or Raisin Bran. You're empty because without her, your life is a mess.

Vivian. Vivian.

One day I take the Jag, drop down to Mel's Body Shop on a whim, I don't know why. Mel hasn't changed. He offers me a joint, a pipe, something to ease the pain.

I see my Ford in his yard.

"You bought my Ford?" I ask.

"Bought it? Christ, man. Ms Redman asked me to store it here."

"You're storing it?"

"Pays me two hundred a month to keep it. Free weed, like. I figured you'd dropped into a pit somewhere. What the hell, Jonny?"

Shoot from Mel's like an addict after a fix—am I a love junkie?—I need her, I need to feel her skin, touch her face, kiss her lips or I'll die. I run out to Santa Monica. To Lassen Drive.

Park.

Knock on the door. Don't care who's home.

Angelina answers.

"Is she in?" I ask.

Angelina lets me by.

She's at the pool. In the sun.

She looks up. Drops her book.

"Oh god," she whispers. "I thought I'd never see you again."

"Let's go for a walk," I say.

She gets a wrap. A pair of sandals. Sunglasses.

We drive to the beach.

The beach has a long winding concrete walk that runs through the sand. The ocean washes up, distant white crests. Calm.

"I can't breathe with you out of my life," I say.

It's a duet.

"I can't live without you to touch," she says. "I'm in a hole. He's completely insane after I came home. Sometimes I think he wants to strangle me. I know he hates me."

"I'll kill him," I say. "It'll take a while. It won't be easy. I'll get him out of the way."

"Jonny." She touches my hand. Silk. "Oh god, I miss you. Don't ever leave me again. Please."

I take her in my arms.

Kiss her. It's like the first time. Home. This is where I belong.

The Bruise

She took me to the loft. She sent Angelina away. We made love. In the loft, I notice the bruise on her arm. Covered with pancake makeup, but the blotch is there bleeding through, a little sunburst of pain.

"Did he do that to you?" I ask her.

"No." She says it too quickly, her eyes dart to the window, to the wall, to the bed, landing anywhere but on mine.

"Vivian, what's he done?"

"Nothing. Nothing."

"That's not nothing."

I take her hand, turn it over, hold, kiss at the bruise that is as sweet as honey. She closes her eyes.

"It's just too much."

"How?"

"I fell."

"You fell." I place my hand over the bruise, the splotchy finger prints match mine. "You fell into a hand, his hand?"

"No. No, but…"

"But what?"

"I don't want to talk about it."

There was a lot she didn't want to talk about, but it was all in her script.

In code.

Once I learned how to read it.

She had tried to break the hammer lock of never finishing in a dozen ways.

She'd taken every class there was to take in LA and none of it had stuck—directing classes from three directors where she learned about angles and retakes and reaction shots, but it didn't show up in her script, and she paid for McKee's Story class three times, but it didn't show up in her script, and she took a couple of method classes but it didn't show up in her script. The only thing that showed up in her script was the pain.

It stood out like a shattered rose.

Little anguished two word utterances subbing for dialogue. Cries for help.

And that bruise.

There are a lot of reasons to kill Peter Fox starting with that bruise and working back to the day he was born. He needed to die.

There in the loft, our second meeting in the tainted sheets of adultery and lust and fornication, I asked her why she didn't just walk out.

"I've told you," she said, "two abortions, his mother plays tennis with me twice a week and I don't want to be a divorced female in LA because then I become one of them. You don't know."

"What do you want?"

"Besides what I have with you? I keep telling you. I want to go to bed with you and get up with you and not have to check my underwear to see if I'm taking some of you home with me."

I laughed.

"Keep the good stuff to yourself."

"Filthy, nasty boy," she said.

That was, I guess, the day I decided to kill him.

For her.

For me.

For the bruise.

The bruise turned blue then black and spread out like a sea of hurt and the bigger it got, the deader I wanted him.

I went back to the Film Institute. Bea didn't like it, but it was what I wanted.

Vivian and I sat on opposite sides of Mackey's class.

From across the room, I watched the bruise spread its poison and I thought about snake bite and how if you suck the poison out of a bite, you can clear it up, make her clean, make her pure and clean again.

You want that if you're in love.

You can talk filth when you're wet and slippery.

You can talk filth over the phone, in the shower, in the car.

But deep down, you want her to be pure and clean so that every time you lie naked with her it's the first time. You owe her that. At least that.

So he was going to die. I didn't know just how yet, or when, but it had to happen.

From that night on we never sat side by side.

It had to be an accident.

Drugs.

Sex.

LA.

Then one day, it becomes clear—This is LA. Senseless violence, exquisite perversion, sin and sex and drive-bys. No end to the ways you can kill a man.

And the big thing—she couldn't know about it. I practice write it a couple times. Burn the script. Then write it again.

INT. MEL'S BODY SHOP. DAY

Mel and Jonny talk in secret.

                    JONNY
          I need a few rocks.

                    MEL
          When did you graduate
          to the pipe?

                    JONNY
          Can you help me or
          not, man?

                    MEL
          Shit man, who am I to
          tell a dude he's
          nuts.

                    JONNY
          And I need a pistol.

                    MEL
          A pistol. What kind
          of pistol?

                    JONNY
          I don't know. A pistol.

                    MEL
          A Glock? S&W? Beretta.

                    JONNY
          Something big.

                    MEL
          What're you after?

                    JONNY
          Fox.

                    MEL
          Fox? In LA? With a
          pistol?

                    JONNY
          Mel, come on, I need
          some help here.

                    MEL
          Taurus. Taurus is good.
          Wide ejection port on the
          45. Nine round clip
          pumpable to 12 if you jack
          down the clip spring. But
          that's illegal.

                    JONNY
          How much?

                    MEL
          A grand on the street, 650
          in a shop but you gotta
          wait ten days and give'em
          a gallon of blood.

                    JONNY
          When?

                    MEL
          Tomorrow. But Express
          delivery is extra.

                    JONNY (V.O.)
          Mel is in touch with the
          finest part of LA's
          underbelly, the part where
          the muscle meets the bone.
          God, I love Mel.

INT. VIA CAMPESINA. NIGHT

Bee stands behind Jonny who's
at the computer typing.

                    JONNY (V.O.)
          Bee can smell another
          woman on me, like a
          cat can smell tuna
          fish.

                    BEE
          I thought you quit
          that class.

                    JONNY
          No, I didn't quit the
          class. I have a
          deadline, so will you
          please...

                    BEE
          I'm sorry. Creative
          artiste at work.

                    JONNY
          What's going on, Bee?

                    BEE
          Obviously nothing's
          going on. But you're
          not here so you
          wouldn't notice.

                    JONNY
          This thing is eating
          me up, Bee.

                    BEE
          It's not any
          screenplay eating
          you.

     EXT. LASSEN DRIVE. DAY

ON a Jaguar parked on street.

Jonny walks into the garage.

                    JONNY (V.O.)
          It's a hot LA evening
          and the smog has left
          its taint in the air.

ON a Porsche pulling into the
garage.

INT. GARAGE. DAY.

Jonny leans down.

               JONNY
          Mr. Fox.

               GREG
          You son of a bitch.

He tries to open the door.
Jonny slams it.

               GREG
          What the hell do you
          want? How'd you get
          in here?

Jonny shoves a wad of money at
him.

ON the bills, all hundreds.
Greg grabs the money
defensively.

Jonny tosses a pair of black
lace underpants in the Porsche.

               GREG
          Hey.

Jonny hands him a baggie filled with crack.

> GREG
> I'll clean your clock, you cock sucker.

Jonny scatters other baggies on the floor and beside the Porsche.

Jonny pulls the Taurus .45 from his waistband.

> JONNY
> Mr. Fox, this is for the bruise.

Jonny jams the Taurus into Greg Fox's face.

O.S. GUNSHOT

EXT. LASSEN DRIVE. DAY

ON Jaguar down Lassen Drive.

> JONNY
> Life experience. Mackey says life experience is the root and foundation of all scriptwriting. Live it, then write it and you can't go wrong.

INT. A COFFEE SHOP IN SANTA MONICA. DAY

Vanna wears dark glasses. Hunched over the table.

```
          VANNA
He didn't use drugs.

          JONNY
He had a secret life.
Men do that.

          VANNA
And the other things.
It doesn't make
sense. A hooker? Not
Greg.
```

Jonny hugs her.

```
          JONNY
It's okay.
```

The Journalist

Growing up is a cataclysm—in two catastrophes—the moment when truth ends and the lies begin. How do you know a man is lying? His lips are moving. How do you know a woman is lying? She's saying "I love you."

You see it in the eyes when the trust is broken—a spring unwinds behind the eyes. There is flaccidity.

Flaccid. A Beatrice word, another big build your vocabulary word I picked up reading her books.

Flaccid. The eyes can't lie when you've been inside her and seen the truth of her writhing as she came shouting your name. No hiding that.

It took all of a second to read her.

Like the bruise on the arm.

A furtive turn away when I said, "Who is it?"

"What?" she said.

"Do I know him?"

"I don't know what you're talking about."

"Vivian, you can't lie to me. I feel it in your breath when you lie to me."

"Don't," she said. Fragile. Cracking. "It doesn't matter."

"I don't care if you sleep with your husband, but when you cheat on me with someone else....Who?"

"If I tell you, you'll hate me."

"How can I hate you?"

"I thought you were gone. I can't live without being touched. He touches me."

It didn't matter. She was right. I'd forgive her for sleeping with him, forgive her for cutting my heart out, forgive her for killing me.

Love does that to you.

A pure love.

But I wanted to put a face on that devil. "Who is it?"

"A journalist." Shame on her face like roses bursting in sunlight. "I'm sorry."

"Where'd you meet him?"

"He's a friend of Peter's. When I came back from San Francisco I went to get a new pair of sunglasses. He was in the office. He smiled at me. I was in agony, Jonny."

"You slut. You silly slut."

"I thought we were over," she shouts. Then falls into an abyss. Tears. Sobs. Trembling. "I hate you for making me do that."

"So we've just had our first lovers' quarrel," I say. "Are you seeing him still?"

"Not now. When he comes over. To see P."

"Okay," I say.

Forgiveness. I didn't have a lever big enough to move her. Didn't own a truck powerful enough to budge her.

One thing I know, I'll die without her and I can't live knowing she's with another man. But a journalist? Not a real writer?

Jealousy.

Forgiveness.

"What do we do now?" she asks.

"Go away."

"What?"

"Go away. You always talk about going away. Let's do it."

"To?"

"Turlock. I'll get a job at a trucking company."

"Are you serious?"

"We can't stay here."

"I can't leave LA," she says. "I grew up here. It's where I live. People see LA as this glitzy movie-land place, but when I was a girl, we went to the movies on Saturday afternoon like normal people, and on Sunday we went to the beach like everybody else."

"What then," I say. "This guy."

She touched me, kissed me, whispered. "Forget him, forget everything but this."

Decisions. I was close to a decision then.

What can you do when you know the only way to pin her down is to tie her up?

I know that if I let it play the way it was running we were through. She needed to be touched. I didn't want anyone but me to touch her.

I was chasing her now.

Afraid she'd get away.

Rules of the Game

Rule One: She wins.

Corollary to Rule One: I lose.

Beatrice smells betrayal on me, thick smell of sex from a distance, the scent of love oozing from my pores.

Late evening, I'm pouting, feeling betrayed, images of Vivian in bed with the journalist as we watch "La Bohème" on the tube by an Australian Opera company—sitting side by side, but I'm not there.

Now there are two men to kill.

Jealousy does that to you.

"What's wrong with you?" Bea says.

"Nothing. I'm tired. I don't understand this thing."

"The opera?"

"Yeah."

"It's about love. Mimi is dying, Rodolfo loves her. He'll lose her." She tears up. "I hate you," she says, hitting me on the shoulder. You don't care about me. I hate you. I give you everything and what do you give me?"

I'm on my feet.

"Where are you going?"

"Out. For a beer."

"I won't be here when you get back."

It's deadly this time. I feel it. Strong stuff. Something in her voice. This is the moment to pull out all the stops. Tell her I'm in love with Vivian, make a break, get free. I look at her. So much pain in the face, hurt, rejection, fear, loathing, disgust.

"Bea...jesus..."

"What have I ever asked from you? Just to be here when I wake up. That's all."

"It's not that simple."

"It's so simple you can't see it."

I sit back down. "La Bohème" Act Five. Tears and weeping. Bea turns her back to me, curls her legs up away from me.

I snake a hand on her shoulder, pull her close. Fake it, I tell myself, fake it, Jonny, you're good at faking it.

She snuggles against me. She's happy now. Simple. So simple. Are they all like that? Just say 'I love you' and 'I think you're beautiful' and they're happy?

If it's that simple, why can't I see it?

Trust.

I feel a hole inside me where Vivian lies naked in bed with the journalist.

Trust.

I see myself in the Commodore with Vivian, naked, while Peter busts his nuts making a living.

Vicious circle being human. He won't sleep with her, I think she's the most desirable, sexy, beautiful woman I've ever seen.

And Bea.

Bea.

Trust. She knows I have my left foot out the door and my right hand in her pocketbook.

Trust.

Four years with Bea and I've never smelled cologne on her. Never seen a love bite on her neck I didn't put there, never.

Faithful.

Trust.

What do I want?

Shit.

"La Bohème" winds down and Mimi dies and Bea cries and all I can think of is Vivian, but I perform, at least as well as Rodolfo. Bea gets sloppy when she's watched one of those slippery romances. She is quiet, takes me quietly but so forcefully I wonder who's running the show.

It ain't me.

I write the scene into the script. Tear it down, put it back together, rewrite it.

Mackey wants to read it to the class.

"You have a natural poetic power," he says, "a kind of untutored poetry of violence."

"Is that good?" I ask him.

"Well, it's not under control but it comes from your gut. If you rewrite it a dozen times, show me Bee's motivation, it might rise above romantic drivel."

"Why do you want to read it then?"

"To show the others what not to do," he says, "but I don't hope for much because they can't extrapolate from your sins to their own. That's why we're doomed as a civilization."

"What about Vivian's script?" I say. "She's got some good scenes."

"I never discuss student work with other students," he says. "Are you going to rewrite it?"

I call Vivian. Feeling guilty. Short of breath. Very loving.

"It doesn't matter, nothing matters except that I get to see you. I forgive you."

"You don't have the power to forgive me," she says. "Besides, I solved it."

"Solved what?"

"P and I will live separate lives, but share this house."

"No conjugal obligations?"

"He pays the bills, I save face with his mother."

"That's a pretty shitty arrangement."

But she wins.

Rule One.

Now there are three of us battling for her.

Poetry of violence.

How primitive does it get—Three guys, the princess and the pea, three dogs fighting for breeding rights.

"What about the journalist?"

"You don't want to know."

I do want to know, but I fake it. Love does that to you.

"Why are you punishing me?"

"I told you, you can't put me on the shelf and take me down when you want to suck my peach juice."

"That's it then?"

She hangs up.

In the script the scene is ugly, unplayable

        INT. VIA CAMPESINA. NIGHT

        Bee on the sofa cries as she
        watches "La Bohème".

        ON Jonny, he's dreaming of
        Vanna.

        INT. COMPUTER ROOM. NIGHT

        Jonny whispers into the phone.

                JONNY
            Are you alone?

        INT. HOTEL ROOM. NIGHT.

        Vanna on the bed talking on her
        cell phone.

        A naked man stands in the
        bathroom door.

                VANNA
            Do you think I'd tell
            you?

        INT. COMPUTER ROOM. NIGHT

                JONNY

```
             Are  you  home?

INT.  HOTEL  ROOM.  NIGHT

Vanna  hangs  up.

The  naked  man  takes  the  phone
from  her,  tosses  it  on  a  chair.
```

At least I know my script is about sin and sex and fornication.
It's the story of my life.

I'm ashamed of my sins, but I love them. I love every last one of them.

Does that make me a bad person?

Loving my sins?

Mackey says, "When did this happen to you?"

"It's happening now," I say.

"A script isn't confession, and I'm not a priest," Mackey says, "rewrite it and change the girl's name."

Mackey is a taskmaster. I give him details, he wants pictures. I give him pictures, he wants emotion. I give him emotion, he wants motivation. I hate Mackey now. But I write for him. I write the scene with Bee dead. I'm killing them all—Greg Fox, Bee, who knows, maybe the Journalist is next.

```
             INT.  A  BEACHOUSE.  CABO  SAN
             LUCAS.  NIGHT.

             BEE  lies  under  a  white  sheet  in
             moonlight.

             She  stirs  at  a  sound.

             Jonny  enters,  a  HUGE  KNIFE  in
             his  hand.

                       BEE
                  Jonny?
```

        Jonny slashes Bee's throat.

Mackey will hate it. He'll say, "He kills her with a knife. Have you ever seen anyone cut up with a knife? No. Blood all over himself. You ever see a severed artery? No. You need details, but you got to get your facts right." I know he'll say that, so I rewrite it.

> INT. A BEACHOUSE. CABO SAN
> LUCAS. NIGHT.
>
> Bee lies under a white sheet.
> Moonlight blackens her face.
>
> WE SEE a smear of blood on the
> sheet.
>
> Jonny enters. He straddles Bee
> on the bed.
>
>   BEE
>   Oh. It's you. You're
>   late.
>
> Jonny places his hands around
> Bee's throat.
>
>   BEE
>   Honey? What....
>
> Jonny strangles her. Bee bucks
> under him. She stiffens and
> goes slack.

Mackey: "Do you want to be a writer?"
Jonny: "Yeah, I do."
Mackey: "What kind of writer?"
Jonny: "The kind of writer people read."
Mackey: "Read? Write a novel then."
Jonny: "But I want to write screenplays."

Mackey: "Then you need to watch *Sunset Boulevard.*"

Jonny: "Why?"

Mackey: "Just do it. And then rewrite the scene. Jesus, when they come to me they're all idiots."

I don't have a choice. God has spoken. I rewrite the scene.

```
INT. A BEACHOUSE. CABO SAN
LUCAS—NIGHT

Bee lies under a white sheet in
the moonlight.

We hear A NOISE.

Bee sits up.

          BEE
     Honey?

A MAN stands beside the bed.

His face in shadow.

          BEE
     Jonny?

Jonny STABS Bee with a curved
knife the kind used by Mexican
butchers.

EXT. BEACH. CABO SAN LUCAS.
NIGHT

The man drags Bee's corpse
wrapped in a sheet to a beached
boat.

EXT. A BOAT ON THE SEA OF
CORTEZ. NIGHT
```

> The man drops Bee's weighted
> corpse into the sea.

I'm afraid to show it to Mackey. I don't want to change the names. The dead Bea scene is still thin. A body in a boat wrapped in a sheet dropped into the Sea of Cortez.

I abandon it. I will never finish anything. Vivian taught me this lesson. If you don't finish, you don't have to own it.

An Onyx Bookend Upside the Head

Once you get an image in your head, it stays there.

Forever.

Dirt. Dirty. Her dirt.

It wouldn't go away, the image of Vivian in bed with the journalist. She was dirty after she betrayed me with him.

"I didn't plan for it to work out this way," she said.

"How did you plan it?"

"For me to use you, but it got out of control. I planned to steal your talent, but I fell in love instead. I hate you for that."

It didn't get any better. I can't see her. Can't look at her. I'm breathless thinking about her in bed naked with him. How can she do that to me?

I pout, try to stay away from her, to keep her out of my mind.

But she's magnetic.

Magic.

I obsess on her when she's there, obsess on her absence.

She wins.

It shows all the time. I lose.

Bea senses the wound, licks at me, a lioness licking the blood from a cut cub.

I let her do it. It feels good. But. I manage a week in the wilderness without seeing Vivian.

Pure hell. Bea wants me all the time. Floods me, keeps me in tow.

I can't stand it with her.

She senses that, tells me she loves me, whispers it a dozen times. Then I turn away.

Loves me like Mimi loved Rodolfo.

Her words are poison.

I want them from only one mouth, Vivian.

I pout like a child, skip class, not about to go there. I'll show Vivian. Show her. Show Mackey. When I don't show up, Mackey won't have them read my scene. Who wins here?

On the eighth day, I call her.

"I'm sorry," I say.

She is hard. "Your 'now you see him, now you don't' routine is, simply put, too draining, creatively and emotionally," she says.

"Are you writing?"

"I'm trying to finish my screenplay."

Silence.

"Let me read it when you're done."

"I don't want to see you again," she says. She hangs up. There is a hole in my heart. Needs major surgery. Won't happen.

Later, I come back to Via Campesina. Bea is at my computer. Crying.

A weird smell in the house.

Wailing. I remember the line, 'The widows of Ashur are loud in their wail and the Idols are broke in the temple of Baal.'

"What are you doing?" I ask her.

She looks up. Eyes red. Hurt. Mouth quaking.

"You prick. You absolute prick. How long?"

"How'd you get into that file?"

"This screenplay. It's not fiction."

"You read it?"

"You prick. Are you going to kill me, Jonny?"

"Bea, don't be ridiculous."

"Who's the woman in the boat?"

"A character in the script."

"You're going to kill me so you can go back to the Malibu Inn with your artsy little slut, aren't you?"

"Don't go there, all right?"

"Oh, we're already there, Jonny. Are you going to slash my throat? In here he slashes her throat then throws her in a boat and throws her body in the Sea of Cortez. You even do it in Cabo. You prick."

"That's one version. There are other versions. I guess I pack up and leave."

"I think you better."

"Give me my disks."

"They're in the kitchen."

"What're they doing in the kitchen?"

"I'm boiling them."

She stands, grabs an onyx book end and smashes the computer screen.

I stand there.

She smashes the computer again, kicks it, rips the cords out of the wall.

She throws books on the floor.

I stand there.

"Just tell me it's fiction," she shouts.

I have a choice. I look at her. She defies me to tell the truth.

"Yeah," I say, "it's pure fiction. All of it. That's not you. I'm sorry if you think it's you."

"It's not art," she says. "I know art, this isn't art."

"It's what I write," I say.

"You go out of your way to hurt me, Jonny. Why? Why do you have to hurt me?"

She's breathing hard. She rushes at me. Mouth demanding. She kisses at me, rips at my lips with her teeth, bruising.

"Take me to the Malibu Inn," she demands.

It isn't pretty. It isn't love. But I get the job done. I'm a mechanic. I'll service any make, any model, anywhere. The tips come in spasmodic rushes.

After Malibu

I guess you can write about love too much then you've gotta take action.

Action.

I knew what I had to do, but I was too chicken shit to do it, I guess because I like steak too much. A man gets used to steak.

When you're high on steak, you don't wanna think about pork chops.

Bea is depressed for a few days after the Malibu Inn.

Ashamed? Afraid? Dunno.

She hides out in the library for days. I come in, find her face in hands. I leave her alone. Take the Jag down to the beach to look at the skin, the waves.

Something happened there at the Malibu Inn.

"I want to watch the sunset," she'd said.

"I want to have champagne and strawberries."

"I want to walk on the beach barefooted."

"I want to sleep naked."

She's got this romantic thing she tries to get hold of with me.

I write it into a scene. Tear it up. Write it again. Show it to Mackey.

He reads it, smiles, shoves it back at me. "Three pages," he says. "Do it in two. Or less."

You screw up your courage anyway you can.

Some guys hit Jackie D.

Some suck Mr. Smokey.

Some snort a line with Miss Cee.

There were things needed saying and I'm too chicken shit to do it.

I guess that goes back a long way to early Jonny in his piss stink bed scared of the night voices and the hammer thud of bodies slammed into walls and the cry in the quiet of the front door kicking shut.

Then, like a mouse, looking out at the heap of hair and bony face and the long abused legs, she's gone.

And I live with Uncle Big.

Never ask where she went, he never tells.

Takes me to school, enrolls me, then goes to play poker at the Royal Crown Card Room.

Uncle Big is a prince of poker. 600 pounds of Poker Prince, a king of cards.

I'm six, seven, other kids play in swings and ride bikes, I sit in the back of the Royal Crown, watch those pearly white hands and the delicate wisps of fingers on the ends of bloated arms—fingers holding flushes, straights, full houses that keep us in the trailer house, food. And I never ask.

Never.

I'm ten, eleven, still watching Uncle Big at the table but now he's only 500 pounds and the arms are skinny and the skin sags off his bones and the other players still lose.

And I'm fourteen, fifteen and have a girlfriend named Jolene who lives in a trailer and wears tight jeans and has been porking guys since she was twelve and we watch Uncle Big now 375 pounds, still sagging at the triceps, still winning, but losing the battle with Big C.

And then he's gone and I've never asked.

Never said those words, "Where's my mama?"

Uncle Big looks like paste spread out in the casket and I'm sixteen and I have to take over, sell things, pay for the casket, 'cause Big doesn't have anything left. I sell the trailer with the mattress that stinks of piss and sweat and I'm seventeen and wild in LA and I still don't know what happened to my mother.

Over Eggs Benedict one morning, Bea asks: "Do you want to know what happened to her?"

"Could you do something like that? She might be dead."

"Do you want to know?"

"What would I do then?"

The eggs go well with confession, images of my mother in yellow. Toast.

I screw up courage, but I can't tell her I need to leave.

Instead I become Juan the Houseboy, cook her filet mignon and grilled Portobello mushrooms and bitter salad greens and Brussels sprouts and I push it into the library on a cart and she looks at me.

"What do you want, Jonny?"

I lay it out for her—the steak, mushrooms, salad. "I want you to be happy."

She sniggers.

She pokes at the filet. Thin slices. The clink of silver on Wedgewood is a musical moment. Counterpoint? Pain.

Blood oozes from the rare filet.

Blood soaks into the roast meat of the Portobello.

A few sprigs of greens on the silver fork.

Then nothing.

"Bea, you gotta eat."

"What do you care?" she smiles a thin smile, thin as a slice of steak.

"You're just hurting yourself."

"I thought we had something."

I wait.

When a woman that heavy takes her time there's gravity in every word so you wait for each one to hit.

"Why do you think I love you?"

"Umm," I say. "Uh."

I wait.

Love coats her tongue, she swallows, her face twists as her tongue struggles with the weight of love.

"Jonny," she whispers, then sinks into the dark hole again leaving me with the remains of a bleeding cut of filet mignon and a gourmet mushroom.

Uncle Big ate spaghetti O's out of a quart can. Restaurant size.

Dinty Moore Beef Stew with a serving spoon, cold.

Two loaves of Wonder Bread. A pack of Ball Park Franks.

A bag of marshmallows.

The filet has tiny globules of fat tucked between the strands of meat. The Portobello turns red with the juice of dead beef.

Love is going to kill me. I write it, later, in a scene, cutting between Uncle Big gorging on Spaghetti O's and Bee sucking on slices of filet mignon.

Show it to Mackey.

"Is this a first draft?" He asks.

"Yes."

"Your verbs stink and I have no idea who she is."

"She's Bea. In my script Bea is Bee."

"She's older than the boy, right?" Mackey asks.

"The boy? He's a man. Kind of. Yes, quite a bit."

"So, is she his mother?"

"What?"

"His mother. Is Bee Jonny's mother?"

I want to hit him, but I swallow the anger, feel it on my tongue melting at the back of my throat.

"No, I don't think she is."

"I think she's his mother," Mackey says.

When God speaks, you listen. This is one scene I don't burn for days. I read it, re-read it, analyze it. Where does he get that?

Mother.

He's right. It's not normal for a 26 year old man to sleep with a 46 year old woman, no matter no matter how good the steak.

It gives me something to worry about while I wait for Vivian to return.

Mackey the Living God

A guy like Mackey comes into your life once. That's it. If you don't hook him there, then, when he's hot, you lose.

Mackey is my god.

I'm awash in sin, a love slut, a money whore sleeping on Bea's silk sheets, but for Mackey I come clean. I write. I tell it all.

Something about words written for a great man cleans your pipes.

Mackey—five words and I see light—says, "I can't see why she..."

And so I change.

He speaks, I change.

He reads, I change.

Never did I ever want to please anyone the way I want to please Mackey.

Maybe he's my father. Maybe he's the man who walked out that night leaving my mother sprawling on the floor, blood on her cheeks.

Can't be.

That guy was a Mexican laborer worked in a fruit camp in Porterville.

"Go hump Jonny's mother" they said. There's a big sign on the wall at the camp, " Jonny's Mother's a hot piece. Cheap."

Then she's gone too. Uncle Big is dead. My father doesn't exist.

That leaves Mackey. He doesn't speak Spanish. Probably never would hit a woman.

So I pray to him at the computer, write epiphanies, scenes, kill, rape, anything for Mackey so long as it's on a page—in the right format.

"Get your god-damned margins right," he says.

I want there to be a god. Someone bigger than I am inside.

Something so big it makes me quiver to think about it.

Something so vast I get lost between thoughts of it and need a guide to find my asshole.

Mackey is my new god. I've looked into him. Spent days tracking him down. But he doesn't reveal anything about himself—to me, anyway. I don't think Guy Mackey is even his name.

"Story, you stupid clot," he says, "story."

I don't mind that he calls me a stupid clot.

I've been called a stupid shit most of my life so clot is a step up, maybe I'm on an upward spiral anyway I used to kick the crap out of any dog who said it. That's why I spent those hours on the beach lifting weights and shoving lard-assed wrestlers around so if somebody calls me a dickwad it's Hiroshima motherjugger and sayonara too.

But Mackey—a lord of words, the king of action and dialogue—well, if he calls me a stupid clot, I must be. There is always room for improvement. I don't expect to be perfect—I could never be the way he is, but I will get better.

I live in the words now. I live for writing for Mackey and I live for writing with Vivian.

She has come to a dangerous place in her script.

The Mafia Don has just discovered that his wife has gone on line and has had a real life (RL she calls it) meeting with her on-line lover and the Don has to decide just how to whack the dude.

I tell Vivian she has to finish the story by having the electronic lover whack the Mafia Don when he busts in on the wife in the bedroom having phone sex, but Vivian hates action in a script. That's why she never finishes.

Mackey read her pages. Called her a stupid rag-rider 'cause he couldn't see the action chains. She cried. I took her bra off. She kissed me. I slid off her thong. We cursed Mackey but just as she came, she shouted, "He's right."

That's the thing about god. You never know when he'll thrust an epiphany on you.

Vivian shot up. She's naked, flushed, got her pad and pen and wrote the scene, read it to me. "Mackey will hate this," I said.

"What is the greatest sin?" Mackey asks me.

"I don't know."

"Not knowing the negative," he says. "You gotta look at the wound not from outside the hard scab—all you see is a scab—you gotta get into the pus, look at the scab from the pus's point of view. You don't do that, you can never write clean. Gotta know dirt to write clean."

I take down everything he says now. In secret, tape everything. Take the tape home, transcribe it. Meditate on the meaning of his words.

One word makes a scene, he says. One wrong word and you lose the reader, viewer, listener. One word.

Mackey is good. He is god to me, good to me.

He is less of a god to Vivian, more of a minor Middle Eastern sand djinn than a major earth-moving, mind-busting god, 'cause she's worked twice with McKee.

"Why, if she's worked twice with McKee," Mackey says, "doesn't she have a story?"

"She has a story about a Mafia Don's wife," I say, "but she can't finish it."

"She doesn't want to finish it," Mackey says, "'cause if she finishes she has to be responsible for it. If god had left the world as a work in progress, where would we be."

"But it is a work in progress," I say.

"Have you ever seen an imperfect sunset?" Mackey asks me. "You ever seen a sinful lion or an immoral squirrel or an imperfect snowflake?"

"No sir," I say.

"Tell me it's a work in progress."

I told Vivian Mackey hated her story and wished she were dead for having worked twice with McKee and still not having a story.

"You're just saying that," she said.

"No, I mean it. He said you worked twice with Bobby McKee and you still don't have a story."

She cried.

He didn't actually say that. I just told her that to make her cry because when she cries the sex is better. Fantastic. She has to work it out.

86

I don't know what I'll do if she ever learns the truth. Cut me off? Castrate me?

She has a pretty good story from where I sit, but I'm not Mackey and I have not seen the inside of a scab yet. I will. When I can get there, I'll be a writer.

I go writing crazy in these two weeks Vivian is gone. Down at the Beach Café away from Bea, away from the distractions of being a kept man. I learned I was a kept man after I read John O'Hara and Herman Wouk—*Youngblood Hawke*—and I wonder what I'd have become if I'd read *The Caine Mutiny* instead, but it's too late and so I write as far away from Bea's bedroom as I can get and still be in LA.

LA is the geographical center of the screenwriter's universe. It is there that the sunset is bloodier, there that the sin is purer, there that death rides a Harley Davidson or a BMW with equal ease at 3 AM, there that you live or die depending on your formatting.

"Get the margins right," Mackey screams.

I make progress when I write alone. I get story. I have killed Greg Fox and I have killed Bee by drowning her headless body in the Sea of Cortez and I'm working on the Journalist who stole Vivian from me after the incident at the Saint Francis Hotel in San Francisco.

I will kill him, but I'm having as much trouble offing him as Vivian is having with her Mafia Don.

Life is short.

Art is long.

I write every day now under the sun and the squawk of gulls washed in the rush of the tide.

I eat only nuts and fruit and an occasional can of tuna. Mackey says there are no satisfied screenwriters because only the hungry dare to look at the inside of the scab, dare to finger the stitches from the point of view of the blood, dare to ride the bullet into the Don's brain.

I am become the bullet, the axe, the machete.

I am become the inside of Vivian's vagina. I feel myself make love to her and I am become Bee's tan and when I killed her in the boat on the Sea of Cortez, I felt the sea slide over her dead skin, felt the first bite of the crab as it tore out a hunk of her thigh.

I am not a prayerful man.

I was not a prayerful boy.

I never prayed in fact until Jane Beggs took me to Mormon church and I learned that I was pure sin and unless I prayed I would never slam her again.

At 15 that's a lesson you don't forget—the relationship between prayer and sex.

So I learned to pray.

But it didn't take. I quit praying after Jane Beggs got knocked up by a Mormon missionary and went to live in Africa and learned Arabic so she could convert Muslims to Mormonism.

I quit praying when I came to LA.

I wanted to come South. I needed to come South. LA is South and LA is where I wanted to go even if I don't know how to sing or play the guitar. Stay out of LA, Uncle Big told me, but Uncle Big is dead and he's buried in Turlock and there's no one left to worry about me, so what the hell?

When you come over the Grapevine and wind down through the Angeles National Forest, you can haul ass. You're on top of the world at 90, 95, 100 keeping up with the Fat Cars—the Saabs and Mercs, the Peugeots and Audis.

You run down onto the flat and it's afternoon and the sun dips its red skin down to the sea and when you get to the Santa Clarita turnoff, you head west to Santa Paula and the water and then just outside Oxnard you pick up the Pacific Coast Highway, a four lane highway that has history written all over it. You see places you've been to in the movies, places from the black and white films of the 40's, places you see in your dreams and then you come to the red bluffs on the East side of the highway, and to the right there's the ocean, blue and wide, and the sun. You know this is where you were meant to be.

I drove through Malibu, saw the houses down on the water like in the movies. The camera takes you inside those places, but I was on the outside and I wanted to go in. I wanted to be in there looking out at the sea and the skin on the beach in summer and the high crested waves of winter time ocean. Don't go to LA, Uncle Big warned me. It's a place where they eat boys like you and shrink their heads after they crush your bones.

But not me.

I had a trunk full of chrome tools and a headful of cars and they needed me down there.

All I saw from Malibu South was German steel and German rubber and German glass and leather, but even German steel breaks and German engines blow valves. In LA there're a lot more of them to blow so they needed me.

I never wanted to go back into the Valley, never hungered for peaches or Thompson seedless grapes, never wanted to drive the long flat highway that ate your tires the way some tooth heavy cat slashes the flesh from bone.

No, LA was home.

It became Paradise when I met Mackey.

Once in a lifetime a man like that comes before you. He is a mystery.

He opened myself up to me.

He is completely unknown and unknowable once he steps outside the classroom.

I would not have killed Bee on the Sea of Cortez if Mackey hadn't told me to get my margins right.

"You're dead in this business if your formatting is wrong," he says.

I believe him.

Two Weeks Dead

Two weeks. She might as well be dead. In New Hampshire with brother, mother, mother-in-law and a phone that doesn't work through layers of family.

I wait.

You wait and dream 'cause what they've got, you want and patience is the currency you use to buy it.

Two weeks. It's like my heart and tongue are numb.

And Bea gets worse, dives into that place where there are no words for me. She sleeps in the library, won't come to bed, quits showering. Exiles herself to the small world of pool deck and library. Even more than before she calls out for things—never wants to go down to the village to shop. No phone calls from her transsexual ex-boyfriend with the big mazoombas.

I learn to use the built in vacuum—an outlet in each room. Learn to run the washer and dryer. Jonny-Juan Kenobe the Houseboy.

I live in the shadows of her exile and she doesn't speak to me. I wait for the two women to open up the locks and let me back in.

I'm cleaning the pool, Bea is on the deck in a white wrap against the hot LA sun, against the burning reflection on the water. Dark glasses. Head lolled to one side. Flaccid. Dead? No.

"Bea?"

Head erect, glasses tugged down.

"Bea, how do you think of me?"

Pause. "Stupid," she says. "I think of you as stupid."

"You're right."

"What do you want, Jonny?"

"Why don't you just send me back to where I came from?"

"You are stupid."

"I don't know what I've done and I don't know how to fix it, and I don't know why you don't send me off."

"You mean why do I keep you here when you break my heart and cheat on me?"

"I don't cheat on you."

"You are a liar and you cheat and you want to kill me."

"I don't want to kill you."

"The script."

"It's fiction."

Dark glasses drop down. Eyes shielded. Lips like fire.

"You have consistently underestimated what I can do for you, consistently hurt me even after I have saved you from your self."

"A man's gotta make it on his own."

"There are no self-made men, they all drive on public highways."

"What do you mean?"

"I mean you are too stupid to know what I mean."

"Bea, have you spied on me? Have you?"

"Darling," she says, "I don't think you are worth spying on. If you were a poodle, I might watch to make sure you didn't widdle on the Persians, but..."

"I'm sorry."

"No, my love, you are stupid. Turlock Okie Valley Stupid."
"So you do want me to leave?"
"Good god no."

Edge of the Cliff

When everyone you know runs off and leaves you, you start looking for something to fill the holes. Dope. Sex. Booze. Cars. Something. Like a '57 Ford. When it's hopeless, just when you think the edge of the cliff is the way out, someone comes into your life like a ray of light.

That was Mackey.

At this time I'm in a long night, I'm a living dildo—I'm a joy boy whore if you don't mince words—living with a rich woman whose skin is tanned thick as rhino hide—living in a house with a pool and driving a Jaguar and hating myself.

Alone.

So alone it hurts.

So, drugs, just a little.

Wine by the case.

Then along comes Mackey.

He saves me.

His red nose tells me he knows something about wine.

His raspy voice talks about fifty years of cigar smoke.

Sun spots on his skin tell stories about the desert.

But what did I know about him after that?

Nothing.

God reveals himself to the sinner when the time is ripe as a six year old Camembert. Reveals it on a cracker and you taste the glory of fungus in cow milk and you believe in miracles.

But what did I know about him after the words?

Nothing.

You try to call him, there is no phone number.

You try to find him, there is no address.

You talk to the secretary at SMFS and she says leave a note, he'll get it.

Mysterious, this Guy Mackey.

So I look into it. Into him.

Scripts. Novels. Articles and script doctor credits as long as his short arm.

But nobody knows where he lives.

I go online, search—there it is—all the facts except date of birth, except place of birth, except name of mother and father, except next of kin, except...

Nobody knows anything about this miracle worker and in LA a script doctor is a miracle worker—he takes words and turns them into images, takes images and turns them into emotions, takes emotions and turns them into words in the mouth of an actor who sticks the emotion right in your heart and says "there, how's that?" Nostalgia, love.

Miracles.

You read his words.

You take notes in class.

He talks to you about your words, but then he disappears.

I check from class to class—see that he wears the same shirt and the same pair of pants and the same black shoes every session.

His socks are always black. Maybe he washes them.

His hair looks like he hasn't combed it in a couple days.

Maybe he doesn't live anywhere. Maybe he materializes at 6:30 PM on Tuesday and Thursday and then disappears, goes off, lives in some electric ghetto with no body and no room. Nothing.

But the magic.

He reads a page of script, points at a word. The bottom falls out—the story disappears. He says nothing, but a week's work vanishes, transmuted into a pile of shit.

Rewrite it, you know, that's that it means. Rewrite.

But how does he know?

Does he have a map of perfection in his head? A road map to the sublime?

He sits for hours in front of the class, eyes closed, hands in a cathedral of fingers—no rings on those pasty white round fingers, no watch on that rail thin wrist—Mackey is timeless—and he listens and raises an eyelid and it's like a hammer slams down and the whole house of words shatters.

"Rewrite it," he says.

Mackey shows up at the SMFS at 6:30 PM as if by teleportation. I have waited in the parking lot, but have never seen him arrive. I go to the parking lot after class, hang out, wait for him to emerge, to go to a car, but an hour later, no Mackey.

I retrace my steps to the classroom—it's dark. No one. Not even a scent of a cigar.

"Where were you?" Vivian asks. "I waited. I about left."

She looks like an angel against the white sheet, the pillow framing her flashing hair, and in the shadow of a bedside lamp at the Commodore Hotel her skin is opalescent.

We make love.

No, we eat one another—two sex hungry people—then we make love and every time I come with her I am a virgin—pure and clean and true.

Sweating, we lie stuck together.

She sighs.

"Mackey," I say.

"What?"

"Mackey, you know anything about Mackey?"

"He's a screen writer that's why we go to him," she says. "Why?"

"Nothing."

"Nothing," she says.

"He doesn't exist," I say.

"What?"

"Doesn't have an address."

"Probably doesn't give it out to keep the nuts away," she says.

"No phone."

"Unlisted."

"No car, no license."

"Takes taxis."

"You can't explain this away, Vivian," I say, "he doesn't exist except on Tuesday and Thursday at 6:30 PM."

She laughs. "Why?"

"Why what?"

"Why do you worry about where he lives? You're here with me."

"So?"

"It's Wednesday. You're with me. Use me."

"Did you rewrite the Mafia Don's death scene?" I ask her.

"Jonny. What is the matter?" She turns on her side. Looks at me. Wrestles a round with Mr. Happy who stands at attention for her. "That's better," she says. "You think too much."

We are slow this time, slow, sweltering in the heat, slide together, skin glue. "Oh god," she says. "Oh god."

Later, I stare at the ceiling.

"Does Mackey have sex?" I ask her.

"What?"

"Do you think Mackey has sex or has he evolved into a perfect being."

"Jonny?"

"What?"

"He procreates every time you learn something from him. Ideas are like sperm—gametes—words are like gametes and when he says rewrite, he must have birth pangs."

"You think?"

"It's an idea. He doesn't tell me what he thinks. I've looked everywhere for someone to help me get out of Act Two. It takes a magician."

"I thought you were rewriting Act Three."

"Oh sure. You can call anything after page ninety Act Three, but where does it really end?"

"Ask Mackey."

"I did."

"What did he say?"

"He said I had a long way to go."

"So page ninety isn't Act Three?"

"He said I had a good beginning but it's too long at ninety pages. He said the beginning should be on page one."

"So he's a perfectionist."

"Hold me," she says. I hold her. She snuggles against me, slides her legs on top of mine. "Mmm," she says, "love the silky feel of your skin." She rubs my belly, chest, face. Swallows me whole.

Mackey reads the hotel bed scene. He shakes his head. Hands me back the pages. Takes off his glasses. Black watery eyes, red at the rims as if he's gone forty days and forty nights without sleep. Lets out a big breath.

"It doesn't fit here," he says.

"I think it's Act Two."

"Maybe," he says. "Maybe. But you don't have an Act Two yet. Rewrite it."

In the Beginning

In the beginning Bea didn't want to go out or bring anybody in because we were at it all the time. We ate a lot of quiet dinners with candlelight. But after Malibu, it's exile and I'm a watcher in the shadows. I call Vivian every chance I get. No answer. I can't leave messages. She's back from New Hampshire but she doesn't come to writing class.

Then, one day, three weeks after the episode when Bea smoked my 'puter with the onyx bookend, I come home, find Bea in a long black dress, hair up, silver and jade comb in her hair.

Regal.

Never saw her that way before. Only saw the money. Only smelled the rich on her like sweat on a race horse.

Earrings. Dangly things down to her shoulders.

Eye shadow—exotic purple the shade of sunset.

And lipstick so rich and smooth you want to lick it.

"Get dressed," she says. Flashes a fresh-painted fingernail at a tuxedo on the bed.

Busy hands. All the diamonds in the jewelry box cloak her fingers. A wrist band of brilliants.

She looks at me, head cocked to one side.

Smiling.

"What?" she says. She takes off the dangly earrings, plugs diamond studs into her lobes.

"Diamonds and high heels," I say.

She raises the hem of her black dress, points her toes.

"New," she says, "got them today."

"What is this?" I ask.

She laughs. "You want to be a writer, it's time you met people who can help you."

The veil has lifted. Bea is back. I don't know if I want her back.

Bait.

A man on a riverbank needs bait.

She flashes like an expensive lure in the water and I am the catch.

I dress.

She keeps away from me, toss the lure into the water. She sits on the bed, crosses her legs to adjust the heel strap on one of the shoes.

Jonny's mouth, wide mouth bass Jonny, snaps shut.

Bea skitters across the surface, a shiny fly.

I never wanted her until she was unavailable.

You take the flesh and skin and lips for granted until they shimmer in a new coat of paint, until the guys at the club cluster round. Then, you're a love-sick pig. A love-pig, hungry.

"No," she says, from across the room as I eye her, mouth lusting at her.

I see the skin-tight black shiny dress glitter in chandelier light, echoes of her feet on the hard glass floor, and under the dress, those legs.

She laughs. They listen to her. She's bubbly and radiant. Champagne in black silk.

My heart pounds a little harder.

Go back a week Bea in the den—a gigantic 54 inch TV—a gift, she said, to help you study your films.

"It's great."

"You don't like it."

"I like it fine."

"What's wrong with me? Why am I so stupid I can't see what's going on?"

"Nothing's going on."

"I know you're lying Jonny. You lie to me when you don't have to."

"Oh come on, Bea."

"No, wait," she's on her knees. "Listen to me. please."

"What?"

"Please. Just listen to me tonight."

I sit. The TV flickers. 138 channels. Everywhere from Mexico to South Africa. I snatch up the remote, snap it off.

Silence deeper than a canyon.

"I won't look like this much longer."

"Where's this going, Bea?"

"You exhaust me."

"What do you want me to do?"

She tries to keep it on track, but the lips quiver and the eyes tear up and she just stutters.

"Listen to me? Just listen to me."

Forward a week—at the party, Bea in high heels, black dress, diamonds, hair done up like sculpture. The goddess of money.

And the people. They listen to her. Where have you been? Mexico? Traveling? We never see you, darling.

I watch the parade. A lot of diamonds.

Back a week—In the den, Bea, blubbering, lists them for me.

The men who came in her before me.

The men who once meant something to her.

The men who betrayed her.

"What is it about me that makes you all cheat on me? Am I such a horrible person I can't get one man to be faithful to me?"

I can't answer.

She tells me about her Daddy, who never was there.

Her daddy who gave her everything she wanted except being there.

Her daddy who went to France on business and sent her mementos from Paris, but never came home for birthdays.

Her daddy who wasn't there when her mama died.

It's a litany.

I listen. Let it soak in. Bea wails on her knees, broken, can't shut it off. "Now this," she says. "Am I so horrid?"

A week later—at the party, Bea sweeps down a perfectly manicured garden allée like a princess. This is her domain, this is where she grew up. First names with everybody reeking of dough.

I shake hands with old men who call her Boopsie and women with blue hair who remember her coming out.

"And you are?" one of them asks me.

"A friend. A writer," I say.

"Have I read anything of yours?"

"No ma'am," I say.

And then like an earthquake. 8.5 on the Richter scale. Vivian.

On the arm of her husband.

She ignores me.

I look for Bea, regal beside French doors. Still ravishing.

And Vivian. In gold and the man beside her in black fitting in, velvet gloves in a suede case, a perfect pair, a perfect match.

And I'm Jonny Wattron and I was born in Turlock and I slept on a cotton mattress that stank of piss until I was thirteen.

Back a week—in the den, Bea on her knees begs, beseeches. Beseech.

A big Bea word, another of the Build a Bigger Vocabulary words I learn from the books until I'm speaking Latin.

She wants me in her life. Can't I see that?

"Why?"

"Because I have what you need. I need to take care of you."

A week later at the party with French doors and pâté de foie gras and caviar and Mondrians on the walls and Chihuli glass on pedestals I watch the two women who tear me apart in shifts and I still stink of piss and I still have my Uncle Big who weighed 600 pounds and I still have a stinking accent that erupts out of me like pus from a squeezed zit sometimes and puts me right in the center of the Dust Bowl.

Vivian floats by on a river of money.

She eyes me, a stranger, but I am not in the eyes and the man on her arm has a small gold signet ring on his left pinky and I hunt for Bea, want to go home…back to Via Campesina. Out of there.

Later, in the bedroom, she undresses, layers of silk and rustle and stone until she's in a white robe and I touch at her and she pushes me away.

"No more, Jonny, nothing is free now. It will all cost you."

"How can I give you anything when you already have it all?"

"Oh, I'm sure you can think of something," she says.

She gets into bed.

"I made up the sofa in the den," she says.

"Bea."

"I'm sleepy, Jonny. My people. First time in a long time I've seen my people. We'll have to do that more."

Later, I call Vivian. She hangs up. I call back. The phone rings, and rings again and the voice says that the number I am calling doesn't accept blocked calls, please hang up, dial *82 and dial again. Bea relents a week later. Lets me in. I'm a naughty puppy who peed on the floor and is punished by exile for a week in the rain. All wet, slippery.

The only thing that saves me is Bea likes sex. She loves it. Loves to be taken so hard her teeth rattle. Loves to be jammed like in mare heat.

And I'm good at it. Very good.

I earn my keep now. Learn to use parts of my body I didn't know had erotic possibilities.

Bea sighs, dangles long fingernails across my bare chest like knives.

"Well," she says, "what else can you do? I'm having people in tonight."

"Do you want me to disappear? Hide in the garage?"

"Oh no no no. Why do you say that?"

"I don't have any French doors in my past."

"You're a pest," she says.

Naked, I see the dapple of cellulite in her buttocks. She tosses her hair.

"I feel so young," she says, "Maybe I'm sucking all your youth up. Maybe in a month there won't be anything left of you."

Getting Her Clean Again

I get an opening the next day.

I call Vivian. The phone rings for a long time. Then Angelina answers.

"Is she in?"

"No señor, she's gone for the walk."

"To the beach?"

"Yes, sir."

I leave Via Campesina, hightail it to the beach in Santa Monica. Find her sitting on the sand.

Crying.

I kneel.

She looks away. Lips trembling, she kicks sand at me.

"You shit," she says.

"I'm here."

"Never when I need you."

"What do you want?" I ask her.

She pauses, wants to speak.

"Just go away," she says, "leave me bleeding."

"What do I have to do?"

She looks at me. Takes off her sunglasses.

Red eyes. Crying.

You never think a woman is tainted when she sleeps with her husband—he has a right, a duty. But when some strange hand has touched her wetness. When she's clenched her teeth in a dark room. When she's arched her back as he entered her. When she's sucked him until he came, she's changed.

She's dirty now. Tainted.

I had to make a choice then, there, on the beach.

I looked at her hair taking the sun, auburn strands so rich a man could retire on them, a mouth so delicate it makes roses and tulips look like concrete blocks, eyes so blue the rivers are jealous.

And I wanted it all.

It was simple.

Tell her she's beautiful. Tell her you love her. Tell her you'll marry her.

It's simple.

I'd wash her off, clean her up, I didn't care if she had gang-banged the entire Los Angeles Lakers basketball team. I wanted her.

I touched her, she trembled. Pulled away. Then, like a hot horse quivered as my hands ran over her skin.

She looked at me. Took in her breath.

"God," she said, "No one makes me shiver like that."

"This other guy."

"I'm sorry. Sorry I…"

"Transgressed? I expect it from you. I expect you to sin. You're you."

"What are you saying?"

"I'm saying."

I hesitate.

"I guess I'm saying that I don't want to run away to Mexico and I don't want to take you up to Turlock. I want to be with you, here, in LA."

She looks away.

She relaxes, a flowerlike beauty nested in her cheeks.

Wind. Sand. Sun.

She soaked it all up in that darkened skin, an exotic woman from an island where only she knew the rules. Only she knew how things turned out.

Love does that.

You give up your hope and you give up your dreams, and you give up planning. With a woman like that, you just give up.

"And what do you mean by that—'be with you?" she asks.

"I guess. I guess I mean I want to marry you."

She bows her head. Fidgets with the sand. Looks up at me.

Smiles.

She's clean now. There is a sunrise in her cheeks and deep pools of water in her eyes and she's washed clean.

"You'll forgive me. That's what caused all this, you know. If you only...."

"Shhh," I say.

"No," she whispers. "I need to say it, you have to know. I can't stand not being touched. I strangle. I choke up. I hate to be alone. Sitting here, like this, alone, I feel like I'm cut off from everything, but when you touch me I feel complete. When you sent me away, it killed me. I needed...."

"I didn't... send. You."

"Shh," she says, "let me finish. I felt like an exile. I had to do something. I hate that feeling. With him it was just sex."

"And you won't see him again?"

"I'm a full time, high maintenance broad," she says. "A one man woman."

"From here on."

I kiss her. The taste of her lip stick is clean, light. Even her lips taste pure. Her mouth.

So it's set. Twenty-six years old and I just asked a 35 year old married woman to live with me.

Talk about changes.

Only one problem.

Beatrice.

My breath is hard as I drive back to Via Campesina.

Crash and Burn

Before you start over, you have to crash. Crash and burn skin and meat to the bone. Then you earn the right to come back.

The Ford. It's what I came to Beatrice with—and my black suitcase with the broken latch—and that's what I'm leaving with.

The suitcase, the Ford and a new woman named Vivian.

But when you've slept with a woman so rich you wake up smelling greenbacks you walk before you run. You don't just walk in and say, I'm outa here.

And you don't just walk out and never come back.

You owe a woman that much after four years. At least that.

But Beatrice isn't just a woman.

I park the Jag. Still smell Vivian's perfume, her body, her sex. I won't wash, won't clean her away this time—reeking of love I park the Jag.

Bea is on the deck. In white. A bikini. A red wrap pouring over her thighs. High heeled sandals strapped up her calves like Betty Grable in an old movie.

How many times have I seen that? Bea on the deck in white, the agapanthus blossoming a blue halo behind her head. Southern California perfection.

The red wrap slithers across her legs, a sea of red off the darkened skin, runs onto the deck.

"Bea," I say. I straddle a deck chair, catch my nuts in the webbing. Stretch, pull loose.

She laughs. "Careful. don't want to snap those boys off."

Surprise. Jovial. Not what I expected.

The knot in my gut unravels a notch.

"Bea, I want the Ford back."

She clears her throat.

"The Ford."

"I know it's down at Mel's rotting in the sun where you left it two years ago."

"Two years? It's been that long?"

Scoops up the red wrap, drapes it over tanned skin, draws her legs up, the white strapped sandals strain against the tan. Backs of her thighs welted by the webbing of the deck chair like she enjoys the pain.

"He says you pay him two hundred a month to store it."

"Mel told you that?"

"No lies, Bea. Why not just burn the thing?"

She closes her book, slips her sunglasses down. Black eyes of a hawk locked on prey.

"I told you, darling, you can't keep a Ford in Palos Verdes Estates, darling. It was you or the car, and frankly, I chose you."

"I want it back."

"So, go get it."

She gives in way too easy. The last time she gave in, she smashed my computer and wrecked my screen writing program and boiled my computer disks.

"Just like that," I say, "go get it."

"Jonny, a stupid car is not worth fighting over. Okay?"

"Okay."

But it's too easy. I'm guilty and it shows. Yes. I'm guilty over anything she thinks to accuse me of. But she never gives up like that.

"What's going on, Bea?"

"One thing that's going on is Mel Burns will not get any more of my business."

"He didn't know it was a secret."

"Oh yes he did. He was supposed to...well… do whatever he does with cars."

"It's not his fault."

"I reward loyalty, Jonny, you know that. A woman needs loyalty and trust. But I can't trust him now, can I?" She smiles. Pushes dark glasses back up. "Can I?"

When a woman gives in that easy, a man better watch his back.

You don't leave your straight razor out in the bathroom.

You don't walk behind a car she's backing out of the garage.

You don't leave dull knives on the cutting board.

When a woman gives in that easy, it's only a matter of time before she whacks you.

From the kitchen, I watch Bea on her cell phone talking, waving her free hand like a conductor. She hangs up. Goes back to her book.

Too easy.

"Bea, you want a glass of wine?" I say into the intercom.

She waves her hand no. Returns to her book. Motionless.

Too easy.

She's supposed to scream—at least scream—and throw expensive *objets d'art* against the wall to show how pissed she is.

I'd let it go but the Ford is a symbol now and I've got to have it. New life. Got to have it.

Bea in the doorway—sneaking up.

"I didn't hear you," I say.

Check her hands for blunt objects.

"Jonny," she says, "why don't you listen to me? That Ford."

"Don't start, Bea, just don't start."

"I don't understand."

"What don't you understand?"

"I don't understand why, when you know so many big and beautiful words, you insist on using those low, vulgar expressions."

"You mean like 'fucking'?"

"Yes, like that."

"Well." I pour a glass of Chateau Margaux, cold, white, dry. "Well."

"You don't know, do you? It's a failure, that's why."

She sets her dark glasses on the counter, lifts up, sits, crosses her legs.

"When you talk like that, it's because you've failed to say what you mean and you're frustrated."

"No, that's what I mean. don't start with your bullshit."

She crosses her legs. "Jonny, have I somehow offended you? Have I somehow hurt you? Made you distrust me? I don't know what to say."

"Well, you creamed my computer and boiled my disks."

"And for that you hate me so much you want this awful sedan back."

"Bea, are you high on something? Let me see your pupils."

She juts her chin out. "No, I'm not high. But when you just have to have this car, this particular car, when there are a gazillion other cars, I wonder what's wrong with you."

"This isn't just a car. It's bored and stroked. Chopped and channeled. It's blown and..."

"Blown. Sounds awfully sexual. Are all men like that with their cars?"

"God damn it, Bea, this means something to me."

"I'm sorry, darling, come here, let me make it better."

"Bea. No suck face until we clear this up."

"So there is hope?" She laughs. "Puffy little Okie white trash today, aren't we?"

"Don't say that, god damn, don't say that."

"You are a writer and writers tell the truth and the truth is you're Okie white trash and you'll always be white trash."

"What if I smack you, Bea?"

"You can't hit an older woman, Jonny. Maybe a hot young slut you take to the Malibu Inn, but not an older woman. Like your mother."

She has me now. Right by the nuts. It took what? All of ten minutes to get it out of her.

"I guess it'll always come back to that, won't it, Bea? But it's fiction. A screen play. A story. A living lie. A waking dream."

Legs crossed, palms flat on the counter top, she leans forward, the white strapped sandals suddenly very sexy, breasts cleft by the strap at the center of the bikini top she says

"No, sweetheart. It's about the car. How much?"

"What?"

"To fix up your Ford."

Switch. Slam. Doors open and close and out comes Bea the Good Samaritan.

"Why didn't you just let me keep it?"

"It's too late to answer that. How much?"

"It's in sad shape. Needs new paint. All the chrome's lousy now."

"Five thousand?"

"I don't know."

"Ten? It can't cost more than ten thousand, can it?" She slides off the counter. "I hate fighting with you. Life is too short. If I sent your stupid car away, forgive me. I'm a woman. I don't know anything about cars. That's why I need you."

She stands about an inch away, not touching, but so close I feel the sun boil back out of her tan. She twists like a cat in heat.

"See? We don't have to fight. Just give me what I want and everything will be okay? How hard is that?"

She closes in, mouth wet.

I wait.

She doesn't kiss me, just whispers at me, "You make me feel so young, like a young girl. All wet and ready."

We're like a machine shoved into high gear. A roller coaster, no brakes.

I don't want it to happen. Vivian is still on my body, dried sweat, her sex, her mouth, but Bea is hard to resist.

Ten thousand dollars. Not a bad wage for an hour's work.

Re-Employment

When you quit working for a man, you judge him. When you want for your job back, you grovel.

Mel is scum of the earth in a BMW. He cheats on repairs and slams clients with salvaged parts while charging for new units.

Love does weird shit to your head. Like I climb out of Vivian's bed and am all of a sudden dying to get my job back.

It's not much of a job, but it's a ticket out of Via Campesina.

Mel acts like he's glad to see me. Shakes my hand.

"Come for the Ford?" He asks.

"Yeah. I want it back."

"It's yers, man, glad to see it get back on the road."

"Mel."

"Yeah."

"I need my job back."

He looks at me like a bull looking at thick cow pie.

"You gotta be shittin' me, man."

"No, I need a job."

"She boot your ass out?"

"No, I'm walking out."

"Man, you're shithouse nuts."

"A man's gotta do what a man's gotta do."

"Steak to hamburger," he says. "What happened?"

"You want the story, it'll cost you."

"I'll bet the price is a slot at the bench."

"You got it." I tell him I met someone else. He looks at me like I'm an idiot. I am an idiot.

"Does she drive an 850 CSi? Boat costs more than my house."

"I'm in love, Mel."

"Dangerous ground."

"Do me a favor, Mel. Anyone asks, you haven't seen me in a month."

The Ford has sweated in my absence. Like a horse left too long without a hoof trim it sags, feels damaged. Hard time under the LA sun where sea air eats metal like termites gnawing through wet pine.

I don't tell Bea anything about the job. For her, I'm there restoring my Ford. To Vivian, I'm on a different road and she's the destination. I work on the Ford for a week, pull the engine, set new rings, swap out the bearings, rebuild the blower 'cause it runs like a treadle Singer.

"Looks good," Mel says.

The Ford, re-built, runs as smooth as a new born butterfly.

"Man," Mel says, lighting a roach, "something in a cold roach just messes me up. Must be the tar." He inhales. "I don't get it, Jonny."

"Nothing to get, man."

"You're crappin' out by the numbers. Hit?"

"No. Yeah, probably I am."

"She's a hell of a woman." Looks at me. "What's she like? In the sack?"

"Smoke your joint," I say, "leave me alone."

Black Bean Sauce

We look for apartments, Vivian and I. We look at houses, we look at bungalows, we look at tents and fourth floor Venice sea-view studios. I have six grand I've hoarded from Bee, stud fees. Vivian locates a small place in Venice—29 Laguna. Three rooms, 1600 a month, beat down but livable if you don't mind ants and roaches crawling over your face at 3 AM.

"You'll have to furnish it," Vivian says. "I won't sleep on a mattress on the floor."

"I'm not planning on sleeping a lot," I say.

She wants me to build a nest. Okay. I'm breaking loose, cutting chains. I ask how she's coming with P.

She doesn't want to talk about it.

Making love to a woman you love in your own place, even if it's on a mattress with no sheets is good, so very good. The moments are ecstasy. Each time is a first time. We order Chinese food, eat it naked on the floor using our fingers.

Boneless Shanghai chicken in an open mouth, string beans sucked one by one clean of their sauce then swallowed whole, laughing.

"What about P?" I say. "What about the house? What about your mother in law?"

Vivian force feeds me tofu in Szechuan sauce, then licks my lips.

"Don't worry," she says, "don't worry."

"Vivian, I need you to be here."

"I'll be here," she says.

Peking duck on flour pancakes smeared with hoisin sauce dripping, juicy, wet.

"Have you told Bea?" she asks. Green tea and fortune cookies cracked open like egg shells reveal our future—"You are trustworthy and honest in every situation."

She laughs. "Except when you're dicking another man's wife," she says.

"You don't seem to mind eating my Hunan chicken," I say.

"Mmmm," she says, "I like it hot and sour. About Bea?"

"Tomorrow, the next day at the latest. I'm about finished with the Ford. When I leave the Jag I'll tell her."

"You love me that much?"

"Vivian Gail," I say, "I'm not asking you to commit here. I'm doing this because I have to. I want to be your handyman even if it's part time work, and if this is what it takes, this is what I do. I want to lick black bean sauce off your thighs, suck duck sauce out of your belly button. If you don't think that will happen."

"You say that, but you haven't done it."

"Done what?"

"Licked the black bean sauce off my thighs."

I lay her out on the mattress, scoop gobs of black bean sauce on her thighs, smear it, and then like a big cat lick her clean while she purrs but then she arches her back and her hands find my hair and then she doesn't laugh for a while.

"That's one of the benefits you get jumping from 800 K a year to a mechanic in Venice. Can you do it?" I ask her.

I hold a strip of Cantonese steak out to her, lift a sliced tomato chip to her mouth, lips red as carmine. She chews. Swallows. Pensive.

"Oh god," she says. Deep breath. And then—"Like when I didn't see you for three weeks, I think something happened to my vagina."

"What?"

"It shrank," she says. "I think I became a virgin again." Another tomato slice, a chunk of water chestnut, a slice of steak. "Because it was painful, like the first time."

"Maybe you have something, woman trouble. A fatal disease."

"No, too romantic," she says. "Can't possibly die right now." I kiss a dark clot of sauce from the corner of her mouth.

"Mmm," she says. "Rice. I need rice. Lots of sticky gooey white rice."

"Tell him." I say. "No sticky rice for you until you swear you'll tell him."

A week of Chinese food, stolen ecstasy, beach walking, jugglers, peace.

"I'm afraid," she says.

"Of what?"

"Of being too happy. I've never felt like this. I love it here with you, like this. We'll write together and walk on the beach and shop at the Market. Oh god, Jonny, I love you. I love everything about you."

And each night back to Via Campesina. And Bea.

I dread the scene.

Take the easy way out, I tell myself, drop and run. Get away fast before she throws something.

But this is the new Jonny, reborn from between Vivian's thighs, a new life.

I park, taste the fear and residual dope from Mel's joint.

I'm set now, got the new job, got a new place, got a new woman.

New woman. You don't just pack up and leave until you've got somewhere to go. It's kind of like cheating.

Alone With Your Baby

One night, just like that, I decide to stay alone. Not tell Bea. Just don't show up. I go out drinking. It's not like it used to be. I'm not hunting.

It's late when I get back to the new place in Venice.

When Vivian and I fixed it up, I was excited. But now, in the dark, it looks like a sun-hammered clapboard beach shack with gray windows.

Inside I smell Vivian. She has marked everything she touched. I'm sensitive to her. She stays in my nose—bloodhound me.

I look at the phone. Wait. Traffic on the street is light. A few voices.

A dog barking. Street light spills into the living room.

Dark.

Shadowy.

Whoooo.

Bea is a case, a hard case.

I take off my clothes. Go to the bureau we bought at St. Vincent DePaul, turn out everything that feels like silk. Closet empties of silk, gabardine, one cotton summer weight suit. Stack it up on the bed. Look at what's left.

Not much.

I box it up. Stuff it in, then start outside when the phone rings. I let it chirp a few times, then pick it up.

"Jonny?"

I wait. Sobs.

"Jonny. Is your slut with you?"

I hang up. Go outside. Set the box on the sidewalk. Hear the phone again. I open the fridge. It's a used fridge that smells like old cheese.

I cap a brew. Taste it. Tastes like shit over the chirping phone. Slam it down. Yank on the phone.

"What do you want?"

"Jonny?" Vivian's coiled voice winds its way into my ear. Soothing.

"Vivian."

"You weren't expecting me?"

"I just hung up on Bea."

Silence.

"You there?" I say.

"What did she want?"

"Nothing. Well. I don't know. What she always wants."

"Oh. I didn't know if you'd be there. I just took a chance."

"You okay?"

"I've needed to talk to you. Will she…?"

"Don't worry. No. Nothing."

"You're sure?"

"Why did you call?"

"Do I need a reason?" That voice. Silk. Sweet.

"No," I say. "You don't need a reason. Can you come?"

"Not tonight," she whispers. "No. He's passed out downstairs. He had a meeting with some money people. I've got a minute. I needed to hear you."

First light, the street lamp shuts down. I sit up, wake up woozy. Half a case of bad beer worms its way out of my bladder. Cold water—face cool. Want to puke. Head for Mel's.

It's a cold coast morning. Fog fits over Venice like a gray steel glove. No sound under the pound of the tide.

"She won't give it up for you."

"I won't let you leave me, ever."

Bombed Out

In America, you feel the bite of chains against your ankle bones. Everybody's got a piece of you. Breaking loose, you feel the locks cinch tighter on your wrists, then you're out. Free. In America.

Most mornings, I get up early, drive over to the new apartment, where Vivian meets me and we make love or put in an hour painting, fixing up something, making the nest before I run to work. It takes me a day or two to work out a routine after I get over the feeling that the world's been yanked off its pivot. You know. You keep waiting for the skin over the abyss to pop and you dive into hellfire and damnation.

PCH that morning was like a dream. Cool. Sunshine. You hear the ocean off Venice, that slow sloughing of waves onto the sand. Slow soothing swish that masks the violence pushing the waves across the sea. The call of gulls.

I am happy.

I have left the woman I love naked in bed, asleep.

I am driving, easy, very cool, feeling the power of the Jag under me, running smooth.

All the way to Mel's. A man with a job. A house. A woman he loves.

But at Mel's I stop at a mess. The shop, what's left of it, is a black cavern full of axles and bodies and the stink of plastic and leather and the thick heavy smell of 90 weight gear oil and rubber burning. There is a tangle of hoses and fire engines and men in yellow coats and hard hats. What hits me hardest is seeing the burned out bones of my Ford. It's gone. Charred. Tires smoldering.

Mel stands in the middle of the highway, defeated, shoulders slumping.

I walk up to him.

"Get away from me, man," he says. "Go."

"What happened?" I ask him.

"Don't talk to me, Jonny. Don't talk. Go away."

"Mel, you gotta tell me what's going on here."

I feel a tightness in my gut. A message from far away digging into me. I know without knowing and when he looks at me, I know for sure.

"It's you, man. You're the plague, man."

"What do you mean?"

He grabs my arm, squeezes hard, pulls me over to the Ford, away from the yellow coats and the red hats. His nails gouge blood from my arm. He slams me into the door. Harder.

"I come here this morning," he says. "A guy is at the door."

"Mel, what does this have to do with me?"

"I'll tell you, asshole." Mel wipes away tears in his eyes. He cries. There's a grimace on his charcoal gray face like the blood is seeping out of his veins and he feels the pain.

"This shark, man, a god damned shark punches me in the chest and he says this is because you hired Jonny Wattron asshole and he flips a switch and the whole god damned shop blows up. It's you, Jonny. You're poison."

He turns his back.

"Shouldn't have took you back. Shit."

My heart beats fast. Too fast. My knees quiver as I punch the Jaguar back towards Venice. To the house on Laguna. The same scene there.

Fire hoses and men in yellow jackets. The red red engines.

Smoke billows out of what's left of the house and there are sticks of broken furniture and glass and books and videos slewed out across the street—dead soldiers in this war I've just lost.

A fire chief kneels at the curb, writing. Men in white coats stand nervously beside him.

"Anyone hurt?" I ask.

He looks at me. "Who are you?"

"I live here. I lived here." Waving at the broken walls, the ruined turret. "What happened?"

"Gas, maybe," the chief says.

"Was anyone hurt? Inside?"

"No."

"There was a woman inside," I say. "When I left, a woman in there."

"No. A couple of people took shards of glass." The chief says. "What's your name?"

But I'm gone. Back down PCH. Pushing it. Down to the beach, and just where Lincoln curves to the highway, I see the twisted steel of a Mercedes and an ambulance, and the black Mercedes upside down in flames.

Oh shit.

Cops block traffic. Three closed lanes. Cars filter down the hill single file to the beach. It's LA. They can't stop it all or the city plugs up and dies. Maybe it's just a movie crew shooting a car crash. Oh Jesus.

Firemen. Not actors. Cops who look like undertakers in their black shirts.

I inch past the Mercedes. Oh, no.

I can't tell.

Can't see the plate.

Can't tell. Don't let it be Vivian.

I turn on Lassen.

Let her be there. At home. Drinking coffee. Smoking. Reading the Times. Anything. Let her be there.

But the Mercedes isn't in the driveway. I pound on the door. A second later Angelina is in the doorway spooked.

"Is she here?" I ask. "Vivian? Is she here?"

"No. I don't see her this morning."

"Is she at the beach? Her gym?"

"I don't know, señor."

"Do you know which gym?"

"No, señor."

I dial Vivian's cell phone. No answer. It rings and rings and rings then goes to voice mail then it stops. Dead.

I know the rest. I felt it the minute I saw the mess at Mel's.

I walk back to the Jag feeling a steel strap around my chest. Breath hard. Eyes stinging.

I sit behind the wheel. No. Can't be. No. I head back to the beach.

Traffic oozes up the hill again. And again I inch past the Mercedes now on a hook and there is a white shroud over a small body on a stretcher on the sand. The cops still look like undertakers and the fire crew looks like a flock of vultures. It isn't a movie crew. No.

I see the plate of the Mercedes and the number is as familiar as my own birthday. The hammer in my chest beats on the steel strap around my heart, a long, slow dirge that doesn't have an end.

On a good day you make the run to Palos Verdes Estates in fifteen minutes. Max.

On a slow day it can take an hour.

It took me three years, six months, two weeks, six hours and twenty-six minutes to crawl through the molasses and syrup of death and I was a million years older and my feet were arthritic and my fingers hurt and my mouth was dry and my heart was a beach ball getting smashed by those six guys who hang out at Venice Beach and throw boulders at one another for fun.

The Jaguar ran like an old clunker. The engine howled in pain and whined its discontent every mile I pushed. My heart pounding harder than the pistons churning in their sleeves. My hands shook.

Beatrice.

She did this. She is the angel of death stealing the last week of happiness from me.

She is the thief.

I parked. Looked at the gray Lincoln in the drive way. Waited. I watched the peacocks prance in the sunlight. The big males, fans like rainbows in the morning light. The brown females strutting, heads down, as they grabbed sunflower seeds from the ground.

And then I went in.

Bea was in the kitchen.

A man in a gray suit, white shirt, black tie, gray oxfords, sat on a stool at the counter.

He wore dark glasses. Pale skin like parchment. No LA tan on that skin. Just the pasty white skin of a man who lived in the dark.

Bea stood at the counter peeling an avocado when I walked in.

"What have you done, Bea?" I asked her.

"Jonny, darling," she smiled.

"What did you do, Bea?" I want to smash her tanned face. Cut her heart out. Make her bleed. Disembowel her right there with the serrated knife she's just used to cut the baguette.

"Jonny, honey, this is Grant. Grant is the architect I've hired to...to redo the deck."

"Um," Grant says.

I look at him. No smile. Architect my ass. "Bea..."

"Forgive Jonny, Grant, he's just an Okie boy from Turlock and he forgets his manners and sometimes forgets how to speak in a civilized way. We're having avocado and tomato sandwiches, Jonny. Join us?"

"Bea. Mel's. The house in Venice? How did you know? The Ford? Why?"

"Maybe we can go over details later, Grant," Bea says. She folds the sliced avocado and tomato into the baguette, slides it onto a plate.

"Yeah," he says.

She hands him an envelope. He opens it, thumbs a sheaf of bills, tucks it into the pocket of his gray suit coat.

"But I don't think we'll start right away," Bea tells him. She slides the plate with the sandwich at me. I want to vomit.

"Okay," he says.

He turns his back to me, sloped shoulders in the gray suit. He slithers away. The door closes. Bea turns to me.

She stands there in her black skirt, high heels, like she's just come in off the street, a red diaphanous wrap over her white blouse like a spray of blood from a fresh wound.

"You killed Vivian," I say. "You blew up my house." My voice is gravel. I can't find words. I am six feet tall, weight, 185, but just then I am an empty, weightless sack of nothing.

"This is your house, Jonny. Right here. This is you. I told you. You don't leave me. Ever. Absolutely not"

She smiles.

"And I didn't kill her," she says. "I didn't touch a hair on her head."

Mourning Vivian

There was a funeral. Weeping women in black ringed the casket. They were family. I was not. They were in black. I was a stranger. Not even Angelina recognized me.

Peter stood in silent shock. But it was fake grief. You saw it in his face as he clasped his hands in mock prayer in front of him. I looked at those hands with their manicured nails. Stiff, stupid, pretending fingers that had bruised Vivian's skin.

In my script I have killed Peter a dozen times now.

In my script I held the .45 to his head and squeezed the trigger.

In my script I buried the blade of a knife in his throat while his Wheaten Terrier whimpered beside his dead body.

That's for the bruise, I told him.

That's for every time your hurt her.

Now she lay dead in a black casket.

The rabbi intones in Hebrew. I don't understand a word of it.

"I'm Jewish," Vivian told me one day in the Commodore. She lay naked on the bed, still pulsing and flushed the way she was after sex. "But I don't practice. I haven't been to synagogue since I lost my virginity the first time."

Their pain isn't the only pain here. Peter's mouth quivers, his hand rests on Marilyn's arm. Vivian's mother. She steadies him.

Under her veil there is probably pity and loathing. And maybe a little fear of what he will do to himself. But she doesn't understand that his grief is a role he's playing for the rabbi and the weeping women dressed in black.

Marilyn says something to Peter.

I'm too far away to hear, but I see him nod, then shudder.

"He hates me," Vivian once said. She lay on the bed in the house in Venice, on her belly, legs up, fluttering like a school girl at the beach. "He wants me dead, I'm sure of it."

I caressed the smooth backs of her thighs. Felt the lotioned seamlessness of her skin.

"No," I said, "he doesn't want you dead."

She rolled onto her side.

"There's insurance," she said, "a lot of it."

"Why?"

"Because of the house. Everything. He likes insurance."

I didn't touch a hair on her head, Bea said as she slid the avocado and tomato sandwich out to me.

Maybe she didn't.

Maybe Peter got even with Vivian. Maybe Peter bombed Mel's place.

He stands at the door of a gray Porsche. It shines in the California sun polished like a newly minted silver coin. He gets in. Closes the door. He drives off. He's free.

I remain at the grave site waiting. For what, I don't know. I've waited for her, for hours sometimes, until she burst into the hotel room panting, hair flying, face flushed with anticipation to collapse on me, her weight like gold against my skin and I kissed that

117

breathless mouth, let my hands flutter over the silky fabric of her skin, and tangle my fingers in her hair. The casket is black.

There are birds in the graveyard. Twittering. Chirping. They don't know.

In my script she still vibrates. Her blood, her hair, mouth. *I didn't touch a hair on her head,* Bea said biting into the tomato, licking her lips.

I stand over the open pit. I want to walk down into the grave, peel the lid off the casket and stroke her cheeks, kiss her mouth one more time. Her small mouth ruby red. I want to run my fingers over the mouth, touch the rose bud cheeks.

"What are you doing, sir?" The voice behind me is ominous.

"I'm a friend," I say. He is old, gray, in black, a silver chain crosses a black six button vest like a slash mark.

He tugs a silver watch from his pocket. Snaps the lid open. Looks at me, then at the watch.

"This cemetery is closed now," he says.

I turn my back on her. I hear a sob. Turn back. He stands, watch in hand.

I want to hear her say my name, but all I hear is the case of the watch snapping shut.

It's late afternoon when I start the Jaguar, listen to it purr. Remember how she sat in the seat, her scent lingering after, and, how, when she had gone, I brushed my hand across the leather to steal her smell from forget. She always wore it. The same scent. *Secret*, she called it.

I drive back to Palos Verdes Estates. Turn down to the beach at Santa Monica. In the right lane, I slow down. Every woman I see is Vivian.

The swirl of a sundress over golden skin. Vivian The flicker of sunlight on raven hair. Vivian.

The glitter of a gold chain around an ankle. Vivian.

The dark glasses pushed up into the hair like a second set of eyes that she uses to peer inside my soul watching every beat of my heart, every thought I have of her.

And then the highway turns and the sun sets, that LA red, burnt orange, like flesh cooked in its own blood and you see the rim of the

Pacific Ocean against the horizon, a thin black line where the world disappears.

I imagine driving the Jaguar into that slit, disappearing, diving into the underworld like an Aztec warrior dying in hope of coming back in the light reborn.

The black Jaguar is a metal coffin. I line it up, point it at the center of the sun and blast down across the pavement, hit the barrier at the beach, spin across the sand crazy spinning and wheel the Jag into the Pacific Ocean, into the dying, blood red Pacific Ocean, and I hear voices. *What happened?* I taste salt water and feel the lapping sea eat its way up my legs and over my chest and over my mouth and I am still churning in the Jag, hoping to die when I feel hands pull at my arms.

A face twisted by water peers at me, hands lift me out and I fight him away but he is big and strong and he whacks my head on the door frame as he pulls me out and I go fuzzy.

Later, I am stretched out on the sand and a face hovers over me.

"Now what did you do that for?" I say.

"You could've died," the face says.

"Maybe I wanted to."

"Can't toss you back," he says. "Gotta keep you."

He laughs.

"Are you okay?" he asks.

"No, I'm not okay."

I sit up. Face the sun. The roof of the Jaguar disappears under waves.

"We ought to call a tow truck for that Jag."

"Screw it," I say, "it's not mine."

"No man, they've got laws in LA about abandoning Jaguars in the surf."

Ferrari

After the Jag is towed out of the sea and after I have been cited for creating a public nuisance and after I ride back to Palos Verdes Estates in the 850 CSi, Bea driving, I go into the house. We have not said a word about the incident. I march into the bedroom.

Bea follows, stands in the doorway. She wears a black skirt cut above the knees and she has on a red wrap—a thin wrap like a cloud of blood over a white blouse. A tank top fits her torso in an obscene way. The top scooped at the neck, the skin of her throat like hippo hide.

"What are you doing?"

"I'm leaving you. This time there's no question."

She laughs. A short burst like a hawk screeching. I look at her. She waltzes around and around twirling and twirling.

In the closet I dive through the rows of shirts and jackets and slacks that all smell of her money, her perfume, the smell of sex on hot afternoons. I lug out my old black suitcase with the one broken latch. She stops her spin.

"You're not going anywhere," she says.

"Stop me."

"Your little angel is dead," she says. Something in the way she says it still takes my breath away. I yank open a drawer, haul out some underwear, a couple pairs of socks, a t-shirt. Just what I came with. Relics. Bones of a dead time.

"You didn't hear me," she says. "Or you've gone stupid again. I said your slut is dead and you're not going anywhere."

I close the suitcase just as she slaps me, hard, on my right cheek. My hand snaps up, snatching hers. She glares at me.

"Wake up, you idiot," she hisses. "She's dead. You don't have anywhere to go."

I close the suitcase. Draw the belt around it. I sit down on the edge of the bed. The phone rings. I look at it. It rings again. Then, silence. Bea sits down beside me. Hand on my thigh.

"No one takes what's mine, Jonny, no one. Especially not a home-grown slut like that."

"You killed her?"

She grins. Her mouth is a gash of red, her teeth an unnatural white. Her tongue flicks at her red lips. "No one takes what's mine," she says again patting my thigh.

"I guess I have to call the cops," I say.

"Grow up, Jonny. You can't fix something like that."

"If you had her killed, you'll go away for it."

"Is that what you want, honey?" She waves her hand. "You really want to give all this up?"

She gets off the bed, leaves the room, comes back with her purse.

"Think, Jonny. You can call the police and you can turn me in, but if I go away, you wind up with what you've got in that little black suitcase. Do you remember when you moved in? I wanted to throw that ugly thing away, but you just had to keep it. I give you everything I have, honey but you won't let me be enough."

She opens her purse, jangles a key chain.

A big red Ferrari symbol hangs on one end, a shiny gold Ferrari key on the other.

"Yours," she says. "A Ferrari and me—or nothing."

"You're a real bitch, Beatrice," I say.

"You can have sugar or you can have money, but you can't have both."

She wiggles the Ferrari chain. The horse prances in the light.

She smiles, slips off her black high heels, drops the red wrap and sidles across the room so she stands in front of me looking innocent as a 46 year old death crone can look in a black leather skirt and a white tank top.

"I'm so tired," she says, "these busy days can be murder." She jingles the key. "What's it going to be, honey? There's the phone. Here's the future." She dangles the key between her breasts.

She stands inches away from me. Her breath coming in quick little pants. She is that way when she wants it hard. She pants and she opens her legs and she arches her body like a cat in lordosis.

"Jonny," she whispers, her voice raspy. "All I ever wanted was for you to be happy and to love me."

She eats the 'love me' the way a vulture tears at a hunk of rotting meat. "That's not much to ask, is it? To let me make you happy?"

"You just killed the only thing I ever loved," I say.

"I didn't mind you pillaging her, Jonny, but this is where you stay. Every night."

She brandishes the Ferrari key at me, a butcher brandishing a flaying knife. I look at the key, then at her face and she has that sloe eyed look that makes me ashamed of women.

"Oh Jonny," she says, her lips brushing my ear. She's on tip-toe, her mouth hot on my skin. "What does it matter now? She's dead and you have a Ferrari."

Her hands lace around behind my neck. I feel the cold key chain, the solid feel of Ferrari against my skin. She kisses at my mouth. Her lips coarse and chapped. She grinds her thigh into my groin. She sucks the air out of my lungs. All I can think about is the Ferrari and a night run up Pacific Coast Highway to Cotati at 150 MPH.

I lean her back on the bed, slide her skirt up, yank her stockings off, feel her skin under my hands, she gasps, and I am hard as a rock and ashamed but I ram into her, she shudders, and I kiss her mouth and for a second I want to puke and she comes screaming and bucking and wet, dripping wet, squirting, she's never come like that before, soaking the bed and then she drops off.

I write it up. Read it. Put myself in Mackey's place—what will he see? Say? Think? I rewrite it. Again. Burn it. Rewrite it. This one feels like it takes my whole life to write it.

```
INT. VIA CAMPESINA. DAY.

Jonny goes into the bedroom.
Bee follows.

Jonny dives into the closet,
tosses out shirts and jackets,
then comes out with the old
black suitcase with the broken
latch. Still tied up with a
belt.

Jonny yanks open a dresser
drawer. STOPS. Decision time.

Then he RAMS underwear and
socks into the suitcase.
```

SLAMS suitcase shut just as Bea
SLAPS him. He SNATCHES her
hand. She GLARES at him.

> BEE
> Wake up. (smiling)
> She's dead. You don't
> have anywhere to go.
> I know everything,
> Jonny. I know about
> the Malibu Inn,the
> Commodore Hotel. Ojai
> and San Francisco....
> (a beat)
> Do you think I'm
> brain dead?

Jonny cinches the belt around
the suitcase, looks at her then
sighs and sits on the bed, life
draining out of him.

The PHONE rings.

Jonny looks at it.

RINGS again.

Silence.

Bee sits beside him. Hand on
his thigh.

> BEE
> No one takes what's
> mine, Jonny.

She pats his thigh.

> JONNY

                    I guess I got a phone
                    call to make.

Bee leaves the room, comes back
jangling a KEY CHAIN It is a
big red Ferrari symbol and a
shiny gold Ferrari key.

                    BEE
               A Ferrari and me
               ...or nothing.

Jonny is confused.

Bee smiles, slips off her black
high heels, drops the red wrap
and sidles across the room to
stand in front of Jonny. She
wiggles the Ferrari chain

                    BEE
               The future.

                    JONNY
               You bought a Ferrari?

                    BEE
               In the garage...
               waiting for her
               master. It's a big
               red, luscious
               Ferrari, Jonny.
               She'll do anything
               you want—fast, slow,
               she'll do it,
               anything you ask her
               to....

Bee INCHES away breathing in
quick pants. She writhes like a
cat presenting to her stud.

> BEE
> (whispering)
> Jonny....All I ever
> wanted was for you to
> be happy...and...to
> love me....

> JONNY
> Love. You just killed
> the only thing I ever
> loved.

> BEE
> I have tapes. We can
> watch them together.

> JONNY
> Tapes?

Bee hugs Jonny, lips brush his
ear. On tip-toe.

> BEE
> (WHISPERING)
> She's dead and you
> have a Ferrari.

Bee rips his shirt open,
presses the Ferrari key between
her breasts and holds the key
between them. She's wildly
kissing his mouth. Raping him
standing up.

FLASH FORWARD

```
ON a Ferrari racing up Pacific
Coast Highway at 150 MPH

BACK TO SCENE

Jonny leans Bee back on the
bed, slides her skirt up, yanks
her panty hose off. Rips his
pants off.

Bee gasps.

                BEE
        Do it, Jonny.

Jonny rams into her.

Bee shudders. He kisses her
mouth.

Then he raises his hands to her
throat and strangles her.

At first Bee is surprised, then
we see an orgasmic smile.
```

Mackey takes his time reading it. I ask him how to end it.

"These things have to get ugly if you do them right. Rewrite it a couple times. By the way, what happened to your friend?"

"My friend?"

"The one you were juicing. What's her name."

"I don't know."

Shotgun

I rewrite. It's still about love. Maybe if my mother doesn't disappear, maybe if Uncle Big doesn't drown in the cancer pool, maybe I don't have this big empty place in my heart.

Vivian filled that place. For a couple months. A week. A day.

Maybe we were destined to it.

I don't know.

What I do know is engines. I can tear down a BMW in an afternoon as easily as Mackey rips up Act Two but it's V-8s are what ate me. I used to think about them all the time. V-6, or a 1958 V-8 engine slammed into a Volkswagen body and how in hell do you make a V-8 sound like a Volkswagen? Flat head V-8s that sound mean like a bull in rut. The sound gets in your blood. V-8, twin overhead cam V-12, in line six.

I'd always dreamed of a Ferrari.

I told Beatrice about my dream—"A Ferrari," I said, "but at 120000 entry level, no frills, I'm not a candidate."

"What will a man do for a Ferrari?" she asked me.

I couldn't answer that because I didn't know.

Mackey takes a look at Act Three, points to the end, the scene where Jonny trades love for a Ferrari.

"Is this how it ends?" he asks. "You sure you want her dead? You can do better than that."

So I rewrite it again and again, burning the pages, getting ready to take it back to Mackey.

```
INT. SMFS.--NIGHT

Mackey's office. He sits at a
desk with a single desk lamp.
He is reading Jonny's script.
Jonny slumps against  the wall.

Mackey looks up at Jonny.

INT. HOSPITAL ROOM.  NIGHT

A clean, well-lighted place.

ON a body in a white bed.

          JONNY'S VOICE
     Maybe if my mother
     doesn't disappear,
     maybe if Uncle Big
```

doesn't die in a pool
of cancer, then maybe
I don't have this big
empty hole where my
heart is supposed to
be.

FLASHBACK

INT. VIA CAMPESINA. NIGHT

BEE and JONNY in bed.

>   BEE
> What would you do for
> a Ferrari?

>   JONNY
> Is this a test?

BACK TO SCENE

>   JONNY'S VOICE
> When you die, you
> want to die with your
> shoes on. A mechanic
> wants to die with a
> set of box-end
> wrenches clenched in
> his teeth.

INT. SMFS.--NIGHT

Jonny leans over Mackey's desk.

Mackey points to the end of Act
Three

>   MACKEY
> Is this how it ends?

                    JONNY
          He gets his Ferrari.

                    MACKEY
          You sure you want her dead?

BACK TO SCENE

                    JONNY'S VOICE
          You don't want to die
          from a shot gun blast
          that takes off your
          right leg and
          scatters your nuts
          all over Act Three.

INT. SMFS.--NIGHT

Jonny looks up.

GREG FOX stands in the doorway.
He LOOKS harried.

                    JONNY'S VOICE
          He looked wild, like a man
          with murder in his heart.

Greg Fox holds a Twelve-gauge
shot gun.

BACK TO SCENE

                    JONNY'S VOICE
          I wanted to capture the
          color of his skin, the
          color of death, on paper.

FLASHBACK

INT. SMFS.   NIGHT

Greg Fox raises the shotgun
like he's shooting skeet.

        GREG FOX
   This is for screwing
   my wife, asshole.

Greg Fox FIRES.

The SCRIPT flies out, scatters
then, in slow motion, is
spattered with blood.

Greg Fox fires again.

Jonny's right leg shatters. His
cock and balls are shot off.

Another shot.

Jonny's right hand blows off,
slams into the wall.

BACK TO SCENE

       JONNY'S VOICE
   Killing on paper is words.
   Dying in a bed is for
   real. You get one chance.

A nurse changes his catheter.

The catheter is spliced
directly into Jonny's groin --
no scrotum. It's as if he's
had a sex change.

       JONNY
   I don't want to die.

       BEE

(Leaning over him)
Will he live?

          JONNY'S VOICE
It's a long white
dream with faces the
color of claret and
voices that wisp in
and out of my ears
like word worms.

The Nurse changes bloody cloth,
replaces it with white.

          DOCTOR
There is reconstructive
surgery.

BEE wails.

INT. HOSPITAL ROOM. -- LATER

Mackey enters. He WEARS an arm
brace.

          JONNY
What happened to you?

          MACKEY
Bastard tried to take
us all out.

          JONNY
I don't remember a thing.

          MACKEY
I have steel where I used
to have bone.

          JONNY
My fault.

                    MACKEY
                    (Pause)
          What're you gonna do?

                    JONNY
          About?

                    MACKEY
          Your script. It's
          hot shit. Now.

                    JONNY
          What do you mean?

                    MACKEY
          You made headlines.
          We came out on top.

                    JONNY
          How did we come out
          on top?

                    MACKEY
          Greg Fox? The
          dumbshit who shot us?
          He did himself.

                    JONNY
          We're a lot alike,
          you and me, Mackey.
          Winners. All the way.

                    MACKEY
          (holding his arm)
          Yeah. Winners

                    JONNY
          I'm not a man.

                    MACKEY

I heard.

                    JONNY
          I piss in a bag that
          a nurse changes twice
          a day and my leg
          hurts, and that's
          crazy 'cause there is
          no leg where there
          used to be leg.

                    MACKEY
          What about the script?

                    JONNY
          You tell me.

                    MACKEY
          Still no Act Two but
          it's got blood on it
          and that gives it the
          ring of truth. You
          know the drill--live
          it, write it, pick up
          your Oscar.

A NURSE enters, shoos Mackey
out then she CHANGES Jonny's
feeding bag. The bag is full
of brown goo that is inserted
directly into his stomach
cavity.

                    NURSE 1
          (inaudible whisper)

                    NURSE 2
          (inaudible whisper)

```
     WE HEAR the whistle
     of machines.  The
     ping of monitors.

INT. HOSPITAL ROOM.--NIGHT

Bee sits beside Jonny, takes
his hand, tries to kiss him,
but can't find anyplace to
kiss.

          BEE
     Jonny.

MONTAGE: images of nurses
changing the catheter.

Grotesque image where Jonny's
genitals used to be.

Changing the feeding tube
buried in Jonny's belly.

Taking his temperature.

Monitors pinging.

A doctor in a doorway shaking
his head.

He WRITES on a chart, hands it
to Nurse 1

INT. HOSPITAL HALLWAY -- NIGHT

          NURSE 1
     What do you do with
     him?

          NURSE 2
```

> Send him to county,
> what else?

INT. HOSPITAL HALLWAY--NIGHT

Nurses pushing a gurney down the lighted hallway and into a dark room.

INT. HOSPITAL ROOM--LATER

WE SEE a vague outline of a body on a simple cot in the dark.

> JONNY'S VOICE
> Lovely lovely Jesus Uncle Big used to say when he won a pot. I'd sit in the shoeshine chairs at the Royal Crown watching his pale white rubber chicken fingers lay down the winning hand. Lovely, lovely Jesus, he'd say, raking in the chips.

SERIES OF FLASHBACKS

(1) Little Jonny on a bed watches his Mother pack a suitcase. She is dressed like a whore.

> JONNY'S VOICE
> I was betrayed when my mother left me.

(2) Uncle Big in a cancer ward. He's skinny. Adolescent Jonny

stands by the bed watching his
Uncle gasp.

>   JONNY'S VOICE
>   I was betrayed when Uncle
>   Big died.

(3) A Mercedes on fire on PCH,
a hellish scene of fire and
smoke and a woman's body.

>   JONNY'S VOICE
>   I was betrayed when Bee
>   killed Vanna. I feel like
>   I'm a million years old.

INT. HOSPITAL HALLWAY -- NIGHT

>   NURSE 1
>   What do we do with
>   him?

>   DOCTOR
>   Well someone has to
>   tell him.

EXT. HOSPITAL LOADING DOCK.--
LATER

Nurses, doctors, orderlies
pushing a gurney into a van.

INT. VAN. NIGHT

Jonny on a gurney.

>   JONNY
>   Hey! Where are you
>   taking me?

                    ORDERLY
          Shut up, asshole.

EXT. A GARBAGE DUMP. NIGHT

A nightmare scene, smoke, ugly
machines grinding up garbage,
men in black slickers wearing
masks, men with shovels digging
frantically at piles of rotten
things tires, crates of
cabbages.

Two orderlies wheel the gurney
out of the van and dump
SOMETHING over the edge.

The SOMETHING tumbles into the
garbage pit.

                    JONNY
          Hey!

The van pulls away.

The SOMETHING lies on a pile of
rotten vegetables.

WE HEAR the thrum of giant
machinery, maybe a bulldozer or
a front loader or a stump
grinder tearing into a hardwood
log.

FADE OUT.

Mackey hates it.
"This is crap," he says.
"What?"

"You need a couple car chases and a train wreck to flesh out this story of sin, sex, fornication and murder and betrayal."

"I don't see how I can work in a train wreck," I say.

I don't want to die. I want to live forever 'cause there are a lot of birds I don't know anything about yet. I've read about storm petrels and studied how the male and the female are identical until you probe their sex organs to find the cloaca.

And I have studied sage grouse and how the male and the female look like different species—the male with his broad chest and brilliant coloring and the female who is a dull and drab prairie dirt brown, so brown she fades defensively into the prairie grass and disappears.

And I have looked at peafowl—enormous turkey-like birds because they run wild in flocks around Bea's mansion—the male colorful with his fantail and the female dull and almost insipid. But birds can't be insipid—everything about them has a reason and a purpose and they are perfect.

I don't want to die because I know—really—nothing about birds.

Mackey says I'm crazy with this obsession.

"Obsessive compulsive behavior is good in a character," he says, "but you're the writer—you obsess you lose a piece of every one of them."

"So what you're saying is that I have to go collectively crazy."

"Exactly as mad as each of them."

I don't want to live forever but I can't stand the stench of the cesspool my life has become.

Where I used to have hope, there is now this sexual darkness.

I remember when sex was white panties and nylons draped over the back seat of my Ford and the smell of a joint and a woman's perfume an aphrodisiac cocktail that said 'again, Jonny, again and again.'

At nineteen, you can do that.

Now, sex is shadow and blood, peeled skin, welts, chains, shame.

And so I write the final scenes, again. A white hospital room, a clean white bed, a figure in white on the white bed, white lights, white. I take a look at what I've got before I write a new treatment.

In death, Jonny in the script will be reborn if he can escape from the garbage pit. Does he survive?

I rewrite it leaving out the garbage pit:

```
INT. HOSPITAL ROOM--NIGHT

          JONNY
     I don't want to live
     forever, not like
     this.

His left hand slides over his
belly to his crotch.

He fingers the CATHETER in the
hole in his groin.

ON the bag full of piss as he
yanks out the catheter.

INT. HOSPITAL ROOM -- NIGHT

Doctor enters, stands beside
Jonny's bed.

          DOCTOR
     We have to talk.

          JONNY
     I don't want to live
     like this.

          DOCTOR
     Well....

Mackey enters.  His right ARM
is in a sling.
```

MACKEY
You need anything?
Anything at all?

JONNY
A new leg, a new
right arm. Fingers.

MACKEY
Prostheses these
days. Miracles....

DOCTOR
Mr. Mackey?

Mackey turns to face him.

WE SEE the doctor married to
the wall, protective white
camouflage--white on white--
makes him disappear like a
white bird against a white snow
field.

MACKEY
Who are you?

DOCTOR
Dr. Von Graf. Are
you the responsible
party?

MACKEY
You mean did I shoot
this cumwad? No, I
didn't shoot this
cumwad.

DOCTOR

> I mean are you the
> responsible financial
> party for Mr.
> Wattron?

Mackey looks at Jonny.

>   MACKEY
> No, no I'm not.

>   DOCTOR
> Do you know who is
> responsible?

>   MACKEY
> For Christ's sake,
> Doc, the man's had
> his nuts shot off and
> his right hand is a
> ham in some mongrel's
> mouth and his leg...
> you can see....

>   DOCTOR
> I'm sorry, but this
> isn't a charity ward.
> We don't know how he
> got in here without
> restitution Mr.
> Wattron will have to
> vacate.

>   MACKEY
> Vacate? You mean
> you'll toss his
> crippled ass out in
> the street?

Dr. Von Graf clears his throat.
Mackey looks at Jonny.

                    MACKEY
          Give us a minute, Doc.

Von Graf disappears into the
white wall. You see just the
tuft of hair at the back of his
head. He melts away.

                    MACKEY
          Kid, what about this
          woman, Bee?

                    JONNY
          Four inches of my arm
          are gone. I can't
          scratch. I don't have
          a dick.

                    MACKEY
          I thought this woman
          was taking care of
          you.

Jonny's left hand slides to his
groin, he fingers the catheter.

                    JONNY
          Fuck.

                    MACKEY
          Did you kill her?

                    JONNY
          No.

                    MACKEY
          What then? She's
          behind on paying this
          two bit quack?

I give the script to Mackey. Habit now. Write it. Show it to him. Rewrite it. Show it to him. The pages, the script, the story.

It's as much his as mine.

Maybe more. I can't tell where I end and he starts. Fine tuning, he calls it. The script is an engine. You fine tune it, it drives you to the Oscar. He hands the pages back to me. I gave up when I had Bea on the bed. I know it. I knew it then. Hands around her throat, I gave up.

When you surrender, they own you. A woman like Bea lives to own things, but things aren't enough. She wants to own your soul. "*You sleep here. Every night. Forever.*"

Mine was cheap.

I go home, rewrite the bedroom scene. Give it to Mackey. He scoffs.

"Your dialogue still stinks."

"It's always stunk."

"Cut the monologues. One other thing."

"What?"

"The Faustian bargain after the Architect kills Vanna? She gets his soul."

"For a red Ferrari."

"That's why it has to be red. It's Vanna's blood."

Now he owns a bigger piece of it. It was mine, a long time ago when I still drove a Ford. But a Ferrari stirs up your head. A BMW 850 CSi pollutes your blood until you think you can't live without it.

Now when I hand the pages to Mackey, my sweat, my blood, Bea's blood, Vanna's blood are on them.

"We'll make a deal," Mackey says.

"What kind of a deal?"

This isn't how I want it to end. But this is the way it will end.

When I let her go, when I took the Ferrari keys, when I didn't call the cops, when I let Vivian die, when I didn't say shit. After that, I'm a shell.

Final Draft

Mackey flutters through the script, catches midpoint at the Hotel Saint Francis in San Francisco.

"Boy loses girl here," he says.

"That's it."

"Boy finds girl on the beach, then loses girl again."

"It's a tragedy."

"The ending is too dark," he says. "I want you to rewrite the ending, leave a ray of light in it."

"I can't."

"You have to," he says. "The market can't handle dark endings just now."

"I already rewrote Jonny at the garbage dump," I say.

"Give me a ray of light," he says again.

I study the moment when the orderlies drop Jonny's naked, androgynous body with his shot off leg into the garbage dump.

I go back to Mackey.

"I've rethought the ending," I say. "This is what I want. This dark ending. It's the way I feel."

He looks at me—suspicious, scornful.

"Jonny," he says, "live it, write it, give it up, but don't dick with Hollywood."

"What do you mean?"

"You've got a female killer."

"She doesn't kill."

"Same thing when she hires it done."

"She just tests the dark," I say, "tastes its sugar."

"Your choice." He hands me the script.

"What?"

"Sell it yourself," he says.

"I don't know how."

"You want a dark ending," he says, "wait till there's a Republican in the White House."

It takes a week. Bea makes it easy.

"Why did you take that class if you don't do what he wants?" Bea asks.

"He owns it if I rewrite it his way."

"So? When did you get your virginity back?"

"Don't do that to me, Bea," I say.

"'Don't do that to me, Bea.' Does Jonny Sugar feel bad about his little lost honey? Take your black suitcase and go home to Okieville and call the cops."

She touches my face. Cold fingers. Cold cheek. Cold.

"It's too late," she whispers. "Way too late to get righteous."

I rewrite it again and in this version Jonny doesn't disappear in the dump. Jonny doesn't sell his soul.

```
INT. BEDROOM AT VIA CAMPESINA--
NIGHT

Jonny straddles Bee on the bed.

          BEE
     What?

          JONNY
     You gotta turn
     yourself in. You
     gotta make it right.

Bee laughs.  Sits up.  Covers
her breasts with a pillow.

          BEE
     It's right.

          JONNY
     She's dead.

          BEE
     That's right.

She opens a nightstand drawer.
Hands Jonny a set of KEYS.

          JONNY
     What's this?

          BEE
     Me and a Ferrari. Or
     nothing.

Jonny clutches the keys.
```

```
FLASHFORWARD

ON a red Ferrari running at 150
MPH up the Pacific Coast Hiway.

BACK TO SCENE

Jonny weighs the keys, looks at
Bee. He tosses the keys back at
her. Picks up the PHONE.

          BEE
     No!
```

I hand it to Mackey. He scans the final moments, smiles.

"She buys it, that's good. How do you feel?"

"What?"

"Do you feel like a man who's going to pitch a story to a producer?"

"Just like that? You can tell?"

"She gets it. She pays. They're going to rewrite anyway," he says. "I might rewrite it myself if the money's right."

"Am I going to be rich?"

"The writer never gets rich," Mackey says. "The script doctor gets rich."

I am empty.

I am nothing.

Back at Via Campesina, Bea is on the deck chair in a black bandana, zinc oxide on her cheeks, a black bikini, a red filmy wrap around her.

She looks at me.

"Oh baby," she whispers, "come to Mama."

I sit on my knees at her side. She rests my head in her lap. Strokes my hair.

"It's so hard to let go isn't it, honey?"

"He says they'll buy it."

"And then you won't need me. Kiss?"

I turn away.

"Come on sweetie, one little kiss."

"I don't wanna."

"One kiss before you get famous."

"It's never one kiss."

She lowers her sun glasses. Eyes red.

"You've been crying," I say.

"I got pepper in my eyes."

"Why were you crying?"

"I wasn't crying."

I stand. She grabs my hand.

"Mackey knows," I say.

"What does Mackey know?"

"Mackey knows you hired the Architect to kill Vanna."

"Vanna?"

"I mean Vivian."

"You don't remember anymore, do you, baby? You don't remember what's real and what's in your script, do you?"

"He knows," I say.

"Because you wrote it doesn't mean it happened. Come on, baby, give Mama one little peck. Just one. Nothing else."

"At least someone knows," I say.

"And you have a Ferrari."

Sex with Bee is an adventure now.

Before it was wild.

But killing turned her loose. Every time I come, I feel her suck more of me out until my bones feel light as a bird's and the older I get the younger she becomes.

One day soon, she'll wake up and be sixteen and a virgin and I'll be the wrinkled old man on the pillow—dusty and shitting his pants. Each time she comes, she gets sprightlier, more nimble, smoother, more flexible, and each time I come I crack another bone, bleed through another chancre, strain another muscle.

And Mackey owns me.

"You look like shit," he says, "you look like something a dog puked up. You look like an old man."

"How's your arm?" I ask him. "Can you sign a contract without an arm?"

"My arm?"

There are two of them sucking my bone marrow, two of them eating me a bone at a time, two of them killing me in pieces.

Mackey is full of shit.

Go fuck yourself, I want to say.

But you can't tell god to go fuck himself when he owns you.

I write Bea dead, half a dozen times.

I shoot off Mackey's arm. I am the white naked Something in the script.

The white naked Something the orderlies haul to the garbage dump.

I am confused.

I show it to Mackey.

"How's your arm?" I ask him.

He looks at me. "You on something, kid? You high?"

"No sir, but your arm."

It was his right arm. I can't remember. But I do remember the shotgun. His right arm. No. Wait. No.

His left.

I write it again. I hate Mackey. He sees deep into the words.

"One word," he said once, "one word makes a scene work."

I remember—'*Get the wrong word down, watch the scene fall apart, watch the audience run for the exits. One word.*'

"This is a game of infinite last chances," he says. "Every word is your last chance. You screw up one word, it's all over."

Left arm? Or right? He's magic. Somehow he's healed up his shot arm.

I hate him.

```
INT. SMFS.—NIGHT

Greg Fox stands in the doorway
a twelve gauge SHOTGUN aimed at
Jonny's face.

          GREG FOX
     This is for stealing
     my wife.

He pulls the trigger.
```

My right hand rips loose from
my wrist.

I look at him.

                    MACKEY
          You crazy bastard.

Boom.

Greg Fox yanks the scatter gun
at Mackey. BOOM!

Mackey spins, rises, falls.

The SCRIPT flies up, spattered
with blood.

It's his RIGHT ARM!
Somehow, magic, he's healed up his arm.
Mackey reads. He laughs. He laughs again.
"So you want to kill me?" He says.
"I really have to kill you," I say.

          INT. SMFS. EVENING

          Mackey opens a desk drawer.

          Unholsters a 9 MM Taurus
          automatic.

          Cocks it, slides it across the
          desk.

                    MACKEY
               Do it right now. Do it.

          Jonny picks up the pistol,
          balances it.

```
He LAYS the barrel against
Mackey's temple.

He PULLS the trigger.  Mackey's
head jerks to the left.

Then it pops like a water
balloon.
```

Mackey laughs. He laughs again.

"Better," he says, "when you kill a man, don't hesitate."

The script shapes up. Deadly. Bea is dead. Vanna is dead. Vivian is dead. Bee is dead. Mel is dead. The Journalist is dead. Greg Fox is dead. Mackey is dead. Jonny is dead.

"Hell of an ending," Mackey says, "I compliment you on nine ingenious ways to kill a talking protagonist. Rewrite it."

I hate him. His entire vocabulary consists of one word. *Rewrite.* Rewrite.

How did he get this far with only one word?

"What's your name?"

"Rewrite."

"Where were you born?"

"Rewrite."

I have absolute reverence for him.

I worship him.

I bow to him.

I hate him.

He is god.

I am nothing.

Mackey owns me —Rewrite—he owns the script. Rewrite.

I cry on Bea's lap. "Baby," she whispers. Strokes my head. "You didn't know what you were getting into, sweetie."

"I'm alone," I tell her.

"I'm here," she says.

"He hates me," I say.

"You need him," she says.

"I'm never writing another word."

"Do you want a blow job?" she asks me.

"What?"

"Do you want a blow job?" She says. "You used to come in my mouth before you became 'un *artiste'*.

"Don't you see what's happening to me, Bea?"

"I hope you didn't put on underwear this morning."

Mackey laughs. "She's a black widow," he says.

"She wants me dead," I say.

"They all want you dead," he says, "your job is to stay alive."

"Sharks," I say.

"Slow down," he says. "Sit down. Sit down. Sit. Down."

His words are anchors.

"You're flying off in six directions at once," he says, "all you need is an ending, for christ's sake. All you need is an ending.

"I'll die first," I say.

"Put your shoes back on."

"I want blood," I say. I hack at my wrist with the letter opener.

Mackey watches me.

I drip, sling, slop blood. It spatters on his desk, on his arm. He looks at me. Dabs at the blood with the tip of his finger, sucks it off.

"Is that what you want?" he asks. "Give me the blade."

Humbled, I hand it to him. He has drunk my blood.

"Go home," he says, "rewrite it. Finish it. End it. Money."

I fall into him the way a small asteroid is sucked into a black hole, father confessor, saint.

"I can't," I say. "She's on the bed with a broken neck."

"Bee?" He asks.

"Yes."

"Is she?"

"Yes."

"You killed her?

"I don't remember," I say. "I don't know. I'm afraid to go look."

"You want me to drive you home?"

"No!" I say. God doesn't have a car. Telekinesis. With him anything is possible. "I'm bleeding."

"Here," he says. He wraps my wrist with a cloth. "Don't spill in the hallway."

At Via Campesina, it is dark.

I park the Ferrari.

Listen.

Silent. Even the peacocks are silent.

The gurgle of the pool pump.

I shuffle inside. Look around.

"Bea? Bea?"

In the bedroom, she lies sprawled on the bed, naked, neck broken, legs spread. "Oh shit."

"Jonny?"

The voice behind me is a knife.

"Oh god, Bee," I say. "It's you."

"Are you all right?" she asks.

I look at the bed. There is no one there. She wears a white sundress—off the shoulder—with a yellow sash around the waist. White sandals. A wonderbra pushes her up like a milk goddess. Her skin is clear, peach, blossomy. She's about twenty. Pure. Clean. Perfect. Wrinkle free.

"Bee. Help me."

I kneel and for some stupid reason I'm crying.

"Sweetheart," she says, "I forgot to tell you. I won't be here for dinner."

"What?"

"I'm going out." She touches at her hair, touches her breasts in the wonderbra. "I'm going out, with a friend, a young …boy…friend…and I'll be late. Very late."

```
             FADE OUT
             The End
```

ACKNOWLEDGMENTS

To my friends who've helped me along the path
I am grateful to all of you for your many gifts of time.

JACK REMICK

Jack Remick is a novelist and poet. You can find all his work here:
http://www.jackremick.com

contact: quartetglobal@gmail.com

www.ingramcontent.com/pod-product-compliance
Lightning Source LLC
Chambersburg PA
CBHW071524170626
46811CB00007B/2941

* 9 7 8 0 9 8 4 0 4 9 3 4 9 *